Step Up To Success

...with Richard Gaylord Briley's life-tested
Positive-Power Pyramid:

Step # 1: POSITIVE PERMISSION
The question is "CAN YOU?" and the only answer is "YES."

Step # 2: POSITIVE GOAL-SETTING
The goals we choose define the kind of tomorrows we live.

Step # 3: POSITIVE GOAL-PICTURING
What you see is what you get. Develop a positive 'round-the-clock' inner movie.

Step # 4: POSITIVE THINKING
Create your own vocabulary of what *can* be accomplished.

Step # 5: POSITIVE ACHIEVEMENT
Learn to assume that achieving your goals is just around the comer.

ARE YOU POSITIVE

"Climb aboard, positive thinkers, for a faster, surer ride on the route you're already taking to success.

Author Briley reveals more secrets behind the power of positive thinking why it works and how to use it more effectively.

Lively, informative and rewarding."

— Marjorie Holmes

ARE YOU POSITIVE

FIVE SIMPLE STEPS TO SUCCESS

Richard Gaylord Briley

WESTBOW
PRESS
A DIVISION OF THOMAS NELSON

WestBow Press books may be ordered through booksellers or by contacting:

WestBow Press
A Division of Thomas Nelson
1663 Liberty Drive
Bloomington, IN 47403
www.westbowpress.com
1-(866) 928-1240

ISBN: 978-1-4497-7436-3 (sc)
ISBN: 978-1-4497-7435-6 (e)

Library of Congress Control Number: 2012921051

Printed in the United States of America

WestBow Press rev. date: 11/29/2012

DEDICATION

Dedicated to the living memory of Arthur S. DeMoss,
who pointed me to a light beyond what I knew... and to
the reader who joins me there.

Contents

INTRODUCTION

W hy do Positive Thinkers succeed so often in life? How are they different—if they are—from the rest of us?

What inner forces took them from what they were, to what they became? And are these forces real, or just a fancy set of words for something nobody really understands?

We can understand the secrets of Positive Thinkers' success by first recognizing something odd about the way life operates on this planet. Nature has a bias. For whatever reason, *roughly half of all optional human activity and productivity seems to be generated by a minority —about 5 percent —of the players.*

Here are a few examples of this imbalance from various fields of human endeavor

Fund raising: Around 5 percent of any charity's regular donors typically contribute 50 percent of its annual income.

Unorganized crime: About 5 percent of all burglars manage to commit 50 percent of the break-ins.

Organized crime Some 5 percent of all taxpayers pay 40 percent of all federal personal income tax collected. And if you add in the taxes their entrepreneurial businesses pay, this minority personally generates the equivalent of half what the Internal Revenue Service collects from all individual taxpayers. (We're talking here about actual taxes paid, not about what anyone manages to avoid paying.)

Play time: About 5 percent of the beer drinkers manage to imbibe 50 percent or more of the suds brewed.

Pray time: 5 percent of the Bible buyers, purchase 50 percent of all the Scriptures sold.

Abundance We Americans, though only 5 or 6 percent of the world population, own the majority (or largest share) of all telephones, autos, computers, bathtubs—and anything else that can be mass produced and sold on credit. We also share that abundance by donating over half the world's total voluntary charitable funds for needy causes.

Most people, including even avid Positive Thinkers, live unaware of nature's *"Five Percent Rule"* which states:

"A 5 Percent Minority Achieves Half of Whatever It Is Any Group Does."

May I suggest that this overachieving 5 percent group has more Positive Thinkers in it (certainly no less!) than the remaining 95 percent?

Positive Thinkers tend to bunch up near the 'success' end of life's ladder. We call them successful because they achieve more than ninety-five out of a hundred do. They may be successful so often only because their brand of thinking leads them to attempt more, persist longer at it, and end up achieving more. In a sense they buy up extra tickets on the game of life, so they end up with more chances of winning.

With these tentative insights, I address this self-help guidebook to that 5 percent of my potential readers who already have a solid 50/50 chance to excel—succeed greatly in life.

Some readers may not know that they have permission to try for success and happiness. Others won't know what steps to take next, even if convinced they were born to be part of the superproductive 5 percent.

That's why this book was written, to rip away the shroud of mystery and misunderstanding that keeps good people from achieving great things in life, things the 95 percent barely dream.

The folklore of the majority teaches that *"If you're rich you can't be happy"*—and vice versa. Disregard this as well-worn propaganda designed to keep the 95 percent comfortable with itself, plugging away inside the system. Much of what passes for common sense in America today is half-remembered, half-digested hard luck folklore imported with our ill-fed immigrant ancestors in steerage.

Poverty and lack of opportunity may have been 'truth' in the old country, but this truth does not fit today in a country whose major problem is seldom productivity, but waste disposal—dealing with the by-products of our national abundance. In this country we've got plenty for everybody. What you earn for yourself does not steal bread from anyone else. And you are not necessarily impoverished of soul and bereft of the spirit of true happiness merely because you figure out how to make a bit of money and live your own life... despite lavish propaganda to the contrary in television plots, movies, novels, and some feature articles written by very young reporters.

Remember, the personal worlds we live in are mostly self-made and self-perpetuated. None of us has to live the way others do, if we find their way of life hurtful or unrewarding. You can choose AND MAKE a better world for yourself and those you love. You have that right, regardless of what others would have you believe.

You have no obligation to use up your years wondering if you really could "make the break' from a dull, profitless existence to a wonderful, productive life. Give it a try. Go ahead and make the break.

You've got the right, even the duty, to kick off any lids others place on your dreams. (Who said their dreams were better than yours? What makes their motives so much purer than yours?)

Use this book as a positive guide through negative environments, to do the following:

1. Gain permission—inner authority—to allow YOURSELF to excel, to succeed in life without the need to hurt others or deny them their chance.

2. Learn how YOU can use Positive Thinking techniques to self-program your mind to reach the goals that are right for you, and good for others.

3. Open YOUR life to the power that comes to all who have a clear vision of what they want to become.

If the life-tested principles that follow on these pages help you to set high goals and reach them and make you a blessing to others and yourself as well while you grow in a renewed and happier life, we'll both be happy.

If these principles enrich you in other ways—as they did me—so much the better.

When you learn the secret, share it with others!

Richard Gaylord Briley
The Lady Blanche House
North Conway, New Hampshire

POSITIVE BACKGROUND

CHAPTER ONE

Life Is Not an Either/Or Proposition

To live is to change. Life is distinguished from nonlife by its ability to respond to what is around it. So as long as you are alive in this world, you will be changing. That fact you cannot control.

What you CAN control is this: HOW you change and the DIRECTION in which you change.

If you do not control and direct your own life, the changes that happen to you will be dictated by others with stronger goal-commitments than yours, or by random events, even things like advertising. (More than one person has joined the Army because of a billboard.)

Your own real wishes may not get considered at all. By simple inattention to your own hopes for the future, you will end up less happy than you have a right to be, less productive than you want to be, less well-off than you might hope to be, spiritually, emotionally, professionally, or financially.

And if that is where you let yourself drift, how can life be any different or better for the people who depend on you, whose own fate is bound up in yours by birth or by choice?

Life is not an either/or proposition. You are not limited to yes/no choices. You can ask for things that no one has offered yet. The abundance of life is such that many times your choices can be both/and. The limits of our worlds exist only in our hearts. That is why it is important for you to assert control and start on the Positive pathway today.

What Are You Waiting For?

Don't wait for things to get better first. Don't wait for the kids (or yourself) to finish college or until you get yourself a new car or pay off the mortgage before you act. Move toward Positive Thinking now, and let it help you work toward better control of your financial future.

Don't wait any longer for one who once loved you to return, or for a divorce to be final, or for the right person to come along before you take control of your life. Start Positive Living today and attract more positive, less punishing, people into your life.

Don't wait until you've got your weight exactly where you want it or all your bad habits neatly under control. Start Positive things first, and you'll learn to handle stress in ways that jolt the body less.

Don't wait to see how the new job or new boss turns out. Don't wait and worry about who gets the next promotion or raise. Start Positive Living as soon as you can, and the best jobs and raises in the future may be yours. (If you even want to keep working at the same old place, once you discover you DO have control of your life.)

Don't wait until you are eligible for Social Security or early retirement to receive Positive Thinking's benefits. *You'll* find no long waiting period before its good influences are felt in your life... once you start. And the payoffs are worthwhile, no matter how long you live.

And that's an important point. There is no ideal age to begin. Only now. For anyone who can read these words, it is hard to be too old or too young to seek the path to excellence along the Positive Thinker's way. Life brings its own reward, and it is possible for most of us to seek a more excellent reward, through what follows in this book, which owes a debt to many who have gone before.

This book is NOT a recipe for burnout. It does not prescribe burdensome behaviors that tax normal people trying to live normal lives. It teaches exciting, logical principles that help *change the polarity* of your living so new and better things can come to you.

There is no good reason to wait any longer. You already have everything you need—inside you—to start your move toward a happier, higher achievement future. You don't need authority from an angel or an authentic million-dollar lottery ticket to succeed. (Quite the opposite. Lotteries' main customers are people who feel they have lost control over their lives. They hope for random magic to zap them back in control.) Life does not work that way.

All you really need for this moment is to acknowledge that something is not working out the way you are now headed. Then turn to the next chapter to see how others have worked out the secrets of Positive Thinkers' success to pass on to you today.

Posi/Thoughts

You cannot control the world, but you can control how you respond to the world.

The
<u>FIRST</u> PRICE
Life Asks You
To Pay for
Something
Is Always the
CHEAPEST!

CHAPTER TWO

The Roots of the Positive Thinking Movement

Two forces shaping the thinking habits and achievements of Americans in the last years of the twentieth century were television and the concept of Positive Thinking. Both came to public awareness and wide use during the same decade, the 1950s.

Television, whatever its content, encourages passivity, imitative lifestyles, and 'take-in' thought styles. It demands immense capital investment to operate, thousands of people to run. It also demands near immobilization of the human body from productive activities so the eyes can absorb moving symbols from a screen.

Positive Thinking, on the other hand, energizes new ways of living. It promotes patterns of thought and action like those that led five centuries worth of bold dreamers, dear thinkers, and hopeful workers to settle this near empty continent and develop a culture that has provided more liberty and more abundance for more people than any in history—and also made television affordable to the masses... as well as networks available to advertisers.

Yet without benefit of billions in electronic hardware or the employment of thousands to feed the system, the idea of Positive Thinking has grown from one man and one book to the point that it has beneficially altered the lives of millions who have tried it, and found a lodging place in the minds of all the rest. Even those whose understanding is somewhat confused know enough about Positive Thinking for the phrase to crop up as standard fare for joke tellers, cartoonists, and editorial writers.

When Norman Vincent Peale published *The Power of Positive Thinking* in 1952, he did better than he knew at the time. To begin with, he was disappointed that the book title he thought he preferred was already in use: *The Magic of Believing.* And it wasn't until a brilliant editor named Myron Boardman pointed out a phrase Peale had repeatedly used in his manuscript, that it became clear that *The Power of Positive Thinking* should be its name.

The great American frontier had officially closed only within the lifetime of men who were still quite young, including Peale himself. The pioneer American epoch of frontiersmen, Indians, homestead farming, railroads, and city planning was still a fresh memory to them. All the hope, enthusiasm, vision, zeal, and drive that had motivated the Bonnes, the Crocketts, and the Sam Houstons of America now resided in their spiritual sons, members of Rotary Clubs and Junior Chambers of Commerce. The ideas that conquered the frontier and settled the continent were taking on new shape, not vanishing with the buffalo herds and clouds of passenger pigeons. They were transmuting into more appropriate form for the work ahead. They were to be reborn as the principles of Positive Thinking.

As minister of the oldest continuously functioning religious congregation in the United States (Marble Collegiate Church was founded in lower Manhattan by the Dutch of New Amsterdam in 1628), Peale had the advantage of a prestigious pulpit from which to operate. He had taken the pastorate at a low point in the church's history. Membership was down, people were moving away, and the economy was bad. These were the dismal depths of the Great Depression of the 1930s and failed financiers had barely quit their well-publicized leaps from nearby skyscrapers.

What troubled Peale most was his perception that businessmen were deserting the church, leaving religion to the women as though the expression of faith were somehow unmanly and to be set aside if one pursued a serious career.

In his struggle to find ways to make virile and real to businessmen the old-time Christian faith he had learned in the small town Ohio home of his physician/pastor father, Peale developed concepts and messages that were to underlie the teachings of his 1952 book. There have been more than thirty-five others since.

As a speaker at clubs and conventions he found early success because the concepts coalescing in his brain found interlocking receptors in the minds of his listeners, the salesmen, managers, and entrepreneurs who were going to get America's economy back on its feet again.

Peak was not alone in pulling building material out of the economic and emotional wreckage of the Depression. Two popular books appeared in the 1930s that taught that the individual was still—despite aggressive new dictatorships in Europe and collectivist leanings in Washington—largely responsible for his own life, achievements, and success.

One book was *How to Win Friends and Influence People* by an ex-YMCA lecturer who had once been traveling advance man for explorer-journalist Lowell Thomas. The incarnation of that author, Dale Carnegie, is still with us in franchised self-improvement institutes bearing his name.

The other book was *Think and Grow Rich* by Napoleon Hill, whose legacy today is found in the bank accounts of thousands of people who took his advice literally (as I did)—and whose entire lives literally changed in a short time.

Hill's unique idea was to interview a generation of millionaires to discover any common principles by which they gained their wealth. He spent twenty years at the task, having been set to it by one of the legendary self-made men of the time, Andrew Carnegie. No kin to Dale, Carnegie was nearly the world's wealthiest man, making his money in steel mergers and spending a share of it by giving towns impressive library buildings that bore his name and dot America to this day. Though he did not donate money for books to put in those buildings.

Applying the same Scottish immigrant canniness in dealing with Napoleon Hill, Andrew Carnegie gave him the idea of interviewing the entrepreneurial rich and introduced him to every wealthy man he knew, though he provided none of the funds for Hill's two decades of research.

These two well-received books were in circulation by the mid-1930s and during World War II. By 1938 Peak had his first book in print, a modest success called *You Can Win,* put out by a religious publisher. It was followed by *Faith is the Answer* in 1940 and his first big seller, *A Guide to Confident Living,* in 1948. It was not until 1952, after a year or more wasted by nervous, unnecessary, and finally rejected editing at his publisher's, that Peale's *The Power of Positive Thinking* hit the market and swept everything before it.

To Peak the editing holdups may have seemed devilish delays, but they later appeared divinely inspired, for his book could not have been better timed in its arrival on the American scene. The economy was climbing and had not fallen back to Depression levels as was widely feared and predicted. People were optimistic about their country and personal future again, despite the ongoing Korean Conflict.

Today, well into the fourth decade of Peale's greatest success, his reputation still towers over all others in his field, and he is no longer alone. But his gains have been conserved in nonprofit institutions like *Guideposts,* the largest paid circulation religious magazine in the world, which he and his indefatigable wife Ruth run.

Ruth also runs the Foundation for Christian Living which publishes *PLUS,* the Magazine of Positive Thinking and maintains a library filled with fifty years' worth of their joint output in print, film, tape, and unpublished manuscript form.

They have mentored generations of America's spiritual leaders, including "Possibility Thinker" Robert Schuller of California's Crystal Cathedral. They have been copied and their success invoked by countless clergy around the world. Giant profit-making enterprises—having no financial ties to the Peales—have adapted and teach Peale's principles along with those of Carnegie and Hill in seminars, video courses, and in print. The conducting of huge Positive Thinkers' rallies has become a business and subculture of its own.

With so many purporting to know enough about Positive Thinking to teach it, one is tempted to quote a long ago comedian, Jimmy Durante, who used to say, "Everybody wants to get into da act."

And this has resulted in lots of unnecessary disappointment. Many people who attend these exciting events listen repeatedly to stimulating tapes by the speakers and read ex-hortatory course materials again and again, looking for the subtle clue or key... which they somehow missed in all the noise and fanfare.

They understand and ardently believe that, yes, Positive Thinking WORKS! They believe other people have succeeded with it, and they will too... when they can finally figure out what they missed, what keeps them from making progress too, what keeps them from getting started right. That is what the rest of this book is about—the SECRET of Positive Thinkers'

Nobody intended to make a secret or mystery out of this, but it happened because too many people were out there disgorging the last lecture they heard, as Gospel to the multitudes, when they should have been silent, studying, and thinking, not pumping audience adrenalin.

All it takes to write a good mystery story is to write a plain good story and LEAVE ONE ELEMENT OUT. The rest of the story becomes a mystery when the reader is not told, say, why the murder victim was done in, or who the mysterious midnight visitor was.

The stumbleblock mystery to how Positive Thinkers achieve their great success is of that kind: something left out, a detail that turns out to be an essential.

Sloppy retelling is part of the problem. Another is that every day we know a little more of the truth than we did before. Older books reflect earlier, more limited understandings. This *a* to all human endeavors.

Still, it may be that, in our eagerness to convince others, we overlooked the repeated discovery that POSITIVE THINKING IS NOT ENOUGH to make Positive Thinking work. This astonishing admission is analyzed in the next chapter.

<u>Posi/*Thoughts*</u>

One of the greatest life-changing forces in America in the last half of the 20th century has been Positive Thinking, with its roots deep in the frontier experience.

Of Everything
Worthwhile,
Half Gets Done
By Only 5 Percent
Of the People

CHAPTER THREE

Positive Thinking Is Not Enough

The difference between Positive Thinking and wishful thinking or magic is a distinction few know how to make.

For until our era, the idea that thinking—an invisible, internal activity—can have visible, external, world changing results, has rarely been accepted by any human culture unless as a kind of magic. Then it was less often looked on as "thought magic" than "word magic" The magical power was esteemed to reside in spoken words, not unspoken thoughts. However, if thoughts had any powers, they were only the evil kind, intended to damage an enemy, not good powers that might enhance life or help to achieve goals.

Part of our problem in trying to practice or explain Positive Thinking is that it is a process, not an end in itself. It is a way to get somewhere, not the destination.

Another part of the problem is how Norman Vincent Peale himself discovered and then shared his then unnamed Positive Thinking principles with the world. Like Columbus he knew the direction to sail. When he landed on the key principles of Positive Thinking, he found better things than he knew. But it was not quite what he first thought he was looking for.

Remember the book *The Power of Positive Thinking* was titled AFTER it was written, and by another person. The manuscript's working title had been "The Power of Faith," though I have heard Dr. Peale in dinner table conversation say he first thought of using a title like *The Magic of Believing* except that a popular book had recently come out with that name.

Nowhere in Peale's evergreen bestseller is there a dictionary definition of what Positive Thinking is. And this allowed a horde of misunderstandings to crop up like noxious weeds which have to be beaten back every so often. That Peale was to be blessed with long life enabled him over the years to clarify his discoveries and correct common errors of understanding. His fundamental good humor and acceptance of people no doubt helped too.

But for years afterward he was attacked by theological precisionists who read their own meanings into his uncomplicated—yet not fully explained—phrases.

So let's say now a few things about Peale's great discovery as it has affected the lives of millions. Positive Thinking is:

- NOT a denial of reality.
- NOT a way of lying to ourselves.
- NOT a confusion of hoping with coping.
- NOT a placebo for failure.
- NOT an end in itself.

From the combined experience of those who have incorporated Positive Thinking habits into their lives, let us then go on to say what Positive Thinking IS.

- It's a way out of desperate problems.

- It's a way to utilize every gift God gives you.
- It helps discern new possibilities, new answers.
- It helps create new realities for your life.

Positive Thinking deals with the real world, providing means to 'see' new realities before they get here, letting you select from life's menu which realities they'll be.

If that sounds a bit overdrawn, that's because of how most people misunderstand Positive Thinking. It's not the thinking itself that does this. It merely energizes the system that you set up to make positive things happen in your life. Nothing mystical about it.

Compare Positive Thinking to the flow of electrons that makes computer chips work. Without the integrated circuitry to do work through, the electricity would dissipate without accomplishing a thing. But run through the right chips, the electron flow can guide the flight of aircraft, search out the light of distant galaxies, or laser a malignancy to save a life. The possibilities are endless. And so are the possibilities of Positive Thinking. But like the electrons. Positive Thinking must be harnessed to a working system of achievement, or it will dissipate in daydreams, disappointments, and lost hopes.

Positive Thinking must have goals. To seek its power without giving it direction is futile. It's like trying to build super roads to nowhere. There must be somewhere to go, something to achieve.

This is the basic misunderstanding about Positive Thinking. It is useless in the hands of people with no goals, no dreams, no hopes. It is the most powerful gift in the world, to those who do have goals, dreams, and hopes. For they are the ones who will make tomorrow's world.

Posi/Thoughts

Positive Thinking lets you choose from life's menu the future that is best for your goals.

GOALS
<u>Are Coordinates</u>
<u>In Time and Space</u>
Which You Plan to Visit
In the Future

CHAPTER FOUR

The Positive-Power Pyramid

Pyramids were among the earliest structures made by man and remain some of the largest piles of stone ever assembled by the race at any time for any reason.

In certain ways, the pyramid can be used to illustrate the true nature and cause of Positive Thinkers' successes in life.

Begin by replacing the common one-dimension a I mental picture of Positive Thinking with a five-layered Positive-Power Pyramid, only one layer of which (an upper one at that) is labeled "Positive Thinking."

Let us imagine our pyramid as having been lost to history, buried by the grime of time and rediscovered in the 1930s by a young archaeologist named Peale. The winds have uncovered only part of the structure and no one can tell how large the thing is, how thick, or how far it is to the top or the bottom. The young digger starts from the highest ground he can find and goes in horizontally, straight from the side, hammer, chisel, and shovel in hand.

He calls his discovery "Positive Thinking" and keeps digging until he comes out the far wall, all the while stringing up lights in the passage he's created, for others to see their way.

Far on the other side of the mound which disguises the pyramid, another digger is cutting a horizontal passage too, but at a lower, broader level His name is Napoleon Hill and the impressive gallery he will spend his life carving out, I call 'Positive Goal Setting."

Like the events at Sutter's Mill, which launched the California Gold Rush a century earlier, the work of these two men drew the attention of others. By the 1950s the shape of what I call the "Positive-Power Pyramid" more or less lay exposed for all to see. Once the excitement of discovery wore off, however, little more was done by others to add to the original hard won body of knowledge. A little rummaging in the tailings perhaps, but no new tunnels were cut. And nobody dug down to bedrock to see what was there.

In time Hill was dead and the lively Peale had many other interests to engage him, though he did sink important shafts down from his level of the pyramid to Hill's, and discovered an intervening layer, descriptions of which filled his later books. He had discovered what I call "Positive Image-Holding,' a means by which goals are retained in the mind as a continual goad to achievement.

Achievement, of course (or "Positive Achievement" as I think of it), is the apex of the pyramid and was recognized by both masters as such. If you were to ask any of their devoted followers the preferred route to achievement, one group would express preference for Positive Thinking, the other for Goal-Setting. (The one group might end up happier, the other richer, only because of differences in paths chosen.) But both methods seemed to work well enough. Nobody thought to look and see if the pyramid had a basement or if there was anything in it.

Until now.

Resting on the bare bedrock of human nature, the entire edifice of the Positive-Power Pyramid is supported by the most basic, elemental Positive Principle of all; *Authority.*

By that I mean INNER authority, permission to step off of Square One, being allowed somehow to get started in a better way of life, cutting the umbilical of inertia.

This is so basic it is most often overlooked. And this "Permission' factor—second only to lack of real goals— is responsible for most failures you see among would-be Positive Thinkers. They start out hoping to do something positive with their lives and end up with more negative feelings about themselves. Somehow, they miss out on the secret of Positive Thinkers' success.

Permission is the key. Ail Positive Achievement rests ultimately on Positive Permission. The stairs to the top start in the basement. There are no guards at the door; only mirrors. If anything seems to threaten you or challenge you at the entry-way, it is only you yourself. No one else can stop you.

5. *POSITIVE* ACHIEVEMENT
4. *POSITIVE* THINKING
3. *POSITIVE* IMAGE-HOLDING
2. *POSITIVE* GOAL-SETTING
1. *POSITIVE* PERMISSION

To enter the Pyramid at the 'Positive Thinking' level, without climbing through the steps below, is to get but a tourist view of the concept—a day trip through a trophy-lined gallery of unattainable knowledge, too quick for one to absorb more than a general impression. *("A nice place to visit, but I positively wouldn't want to live there.")*

The best many can do is make photos of a few helpful slogans seen on the walls and put them away to rediscover in some old album the next time they move.

Those who successfully absorbed Positive Thinking methodology before us all went through each of the five steps listed above, often, we know, without recognizing exactly what they were doing, operating intuitively yet correctly.

The obvious logic to the Pyramid may satisfy many readers, who will need look no further for the reason they did not succeed earlier. But closer study is required to see why "PERMISSION" is so important for many would-be Pyramid climbers. That will be done in the next chapter.

Working down from the tip of the Pyramid, there is no argument that the purpose of all our endeavor is to do something, to make some positive achievement, whether it be achieving simple personal happiness or creating some complex project.

Positive Thinking, the next layer down, is the means by which achievement is made. It is underlaid in turn by Positive Image-Holding, a kind of road map to achievement. And it is dependent on Positive Goal-Setting, the choosing of the achievements to be made. Underlying it all is Positive Permission, authorizing the entire enterprise.

The Computer Analogy

Or, to change the analogy from stone to silicon and compare the process not to a pyramid but to a computer, then:

The computer's on/off switch is *Positive Permission.*
The computer keyboard is *Positive Goal-Setting.*
The computer screen is *Positive Image-Holding.*
The computer program is *Positive Thinking.*
The computer output is *Positive Achievement*

If there is one single "secret" to Positive Thinkers' success, it has to be the role of "PERMISSION" as the on/off switch to the computer. How many people have fruitlessly frittered away precious life, fingering an unresponsive keyboard and looking for light from a darkened screen? No one ever told them before to look for a switch. They thought the only thing that had to be turned on was themselves.

Let's say it again, another way: Failure to understand the fundamental importance of "Permission" is the chief obstacle to getting started on the path to Positive Achievement.

It may be thought that I have done injustice to the well-known writings of others, including W. Clement Stone, the man behind the philosophy of "PMA" ("Positive Mental Attitude") and Robert Schuller, expositor of "Possibility Thinking," by not allotting them separate levels in the pyramid. However, lengthy examination of their teachings suggests the same conclusion as a quick glance. They are students of Norman Vincent Peale for the most part, and good ones. Both market the same positive product under distinctive brand names to appeal to different audiences—Stone to young salesmen and professional motivators, Schuller to older-age television viewers.

Stone has the distinction of having supported the work of Napoleon Hill during Hill's lifetime, co-authoring PMA books with him that continue to have wide readership and influence. A man whose Positive preaching and practice coincide. Stone will always be identified by those whose lives he affected with Success magazine and the giant Positive Thinkers rallies he helped organize.

However helpful the teachings of these two men and others less famous but no less active, they do not help us at this moment in our discussion of the "secret" of Positive Thinkers; success. But the next chapter does.

Posi/Thoughts

You are part of the first generation to understand that Positive Thinking is made up of five simple elements, and the overlooked key element is Positive Permission—accepting inner authority to climb the pyramid of success.

Five Simple Steps
to Positive Thinkers'
Success

CHAPTER FIVE

STEP ONE
Positive Permission:
What Stands in Your Way?

We may pity the Russian people and others who live in societies where freedom of movement is restricted by the use of internal passports. Without the proper piece of paper in hand, they are locked in place, unable to move away, unable to take another job, unable to improve their lot in life. But let us spare some sympathy as well for those who live in our own, freer Western society, who are as locked in place as any malcontented Muscovite. They lack the right credentials, they think, to grant them permission to be somewhere else, doing something better with their lives.

"Credentialism"—the demand for documents as tokens of achievement, obedience, passive endurance, and status—seems ready to overrun the individual, no matter what part of the globe you visit.

And it's growing worse. In our personal dealings with government bodies and too many corporations, most of us have experienced bureaucratic abuses and distortions where the credential, the mere paper, becomes more real, more important to the mindless machinery, than the person—the very creature of God—who carries it. One need have no apology for absorbing the self-destructive idea that he or she is not worth much without the authentication provided by credentials. This wrong-headed notion compounds the problem many of us already have in getting permission from *ourselves* (much less some arrogant outside authority) to BE ourselves.

At first thought, "permission" should not be a special problem. Isn't everybody free to do their best, be their best, try their best? Won't talent and ability just naturally rise, like cream in a bottle, to the top?

Well, no, in fact. Not in a homogenized society like ours where milk itself is treated to keep its meager cream content from rising.

It's been well said by the poets. *'Of all the words of tongue or pen, the saddest are these; What might have* been.' Until ability, talent, and energy are released by some inner or outer "authority," life remains only "what might have been.*

Most of us live so far within the range of our abilities that we never see the fences, if there are any. We do not have permission to be any better than our original surroundings or to surpass the people we accidentally find around us. To do so would be somehow disloyal (to what, we've never asked). We are not allowed to pursue great challenges because it is written somewhere in our souls that we have not the right to do so. Or so we think.

Positive Thinking and all that goes with it is without value if one has no permission to try it or apply it.

We are born, as someone has put it, 'half animal and half symbol." Man is a tool-using, goal-directed, problem-solving, symbol-manipulating creature. We spend so many of our early years in learning the meaning of our symbols, we easily confuse them with the reality they speak of. In the process of adapting the "animal" to the culture into which we are born, so many restrictions are forced upon us it can take a lifetime to work beyond them. (A main function of mental health workers, in fact, is helping people undo damage left over from problems of childhood adjustment to the outside world.)

Even without problems to overcome, all of us seem to need authorization from some source or another before we venture out into the larger world. Without "permission" most of us would languish inside the open gate of life, fearful to step very far outside. It's easy to accept the "givens"—the demands and assumed limits—of our society and never know what we are truly permitted by our nature, our gifts, our talents, our God to do. "Permission" frees us to explore all the potential of this exciting world.

Permission (or greatness or simply better things in life can come in many ways. But without that permission to freely range forth and face the greater world, we will pursue no unpermitted dreams. Even Positive Thinking cannot give you inner permission you do not already have.

The Hunger for Permission

For the purpose of this book, I define Permission as *"A ritual that grants authority for a change in behavior."*

It matters not, in most cases, the exact source of the ritual authority; it is only a trigger that releases pre-existing, untouched energy sources. This triggering can be inner-generated; it may be outer-imposed. Behind the change in behavior we seek is some sort of ritual that breaks the skin of restraint and allows new human hopes to blossom forth, new human possibilities to flourish.

Two centuries ago this book in your hand—or any book— could not legally have found an audience without the permission granted its opinions by some powerful patron (Lord or Lady Somebody) to whom the book was dedicated.

Even the Book of Books, the Holy Bible, God's Word if you will, needed permission to get published. It came to us in English in the famous "Authorized Version" dedicated to King James I of England in 1611, who "appointed [it] to be read in churches." By definition, any other version of the Bible was UNauthorized, its publisher certain of trouble.

By this social demand for permission or authority to publish (plus a convenient tax on paper) the ruling establishment of the time required its approval before a book could be printed or read. That the flow of new ideas was thereby restricted was surely no unintentional effect. Without the permission granted by new ideas, most people would stay neatly in the well-defined social class into which they were born, without all that messy class climbing and trying to get rich and act like their betters. Don't think the ruling classes of the past didn't know about the Power of Permission. You can see they did.

The key thing was the permission. It was not enough for a writer to find INNER authority to put his words down. The reading public had to have official permission to read the words once he wrote them. Attention to little niceties like these explains continuing above average literacy rates in Siberian prison camps to our own day.

As far back as you go in the history of our race, you find the continual evidence of permission seeking before launching out on great endeavors or responding to great challenges. In a straight line of tradition from Babylonian priests three millennia ago to today's commissars and capitalists, no major public building can be erected without a cornerstone laying ceremony. This is a permission ritual of the first order, invoking success for the builders and peace for the occupants. (The Babylonian ceremony was a little more direct so their deities could not misread the intention. It was customary to kill firstborn children and random workers, placing their bodies in the foundations as offerings to assure that the gods would not view the new structure as an affront to their honor.)

Likewise, every ship ever launched with a baptismal bottle of champagne replayed ancient permission rituals. The shipbuilders sought to pre-wet the hull, hoping to placate the easily-angered sea gods with an offering of alcohol, that they might not choose to swallow up the ship and those who sailed her.

The Native Americans who planted a dead fish in each hill of corn and squash did so with the practical effect of providing fertilizer, but for the purpose of pleasing the Com Goddess, gaining her permission to irritate the Earth with their agricultural implements.

The world-conquering Romans maintained important officials on the public payroll whose job was to determine whether the senate and people of Rome had permission from their gods to embark on a given course of action at a given time. They studied the skies to see which way the birds were flying, or killed animals ceremonially so the innards could be examined while warm to discern the permission patterns of the patron gods. Only then, with permission granted from on high, could the mighty legions of Rome march.

Another legacy which the Romans passed on to us came straight from the earliest days of Babylon: astrology. How many people (mostly 95 percenters, I presume) read this morning's newspaper only to learn if the stars would permit them to enjoy the day?

Ceremony As Permission

All ceremonies are permission-seeking events.

Marriage is a ceremony that grants sexual permission. (It's what gives the "consent" to consenting adults. It also gives society's consent to their having children.) The ceremony of kissing the bride (never the groom) is the society's way of assenting to the woman's future lack of availability to those doing the kissing.

Oath taking in court grants one permission to tell the whole truth as one sees it, with theoretical protection from the consequences. Military induction ceremonies grant permission to kill people wearing other uniforms.

The legends of the Mafia and crime lord godfathers gain much of their power and public fascination from the rituals and ceremony associated with them, which distinguish their criminality from the garden variety. To be threatened by a common criminal could be upsetting, but to be kissed on the cheek by the "godfather," knowing full well it marked one for extinction by the mob, could be almost paralyzing, so great is the power of ceremony!

The ritual of education, together with the ceremony of graduation which grants a valuable credential, gives the graduate permission to seek employment at certain levels of income and in certain lines of work. The credential grants the employer permission to hire also.

Taking the oath of citizenship is a ceremony that authorizes one to reject a former life, with its problems, and attempt to attain something better—often starting with a new name uncontaminated by the problems that hung on the old.

Permission by Authority

A common way to acquire "permission" as I mean it, is through approval by established authority. In business this can mean purchasing a franchise which, among other benefits, confers 'permission' to engage in that business for profit. Without this unspoken authorization behind them some franchisees might never go into business. They dc not have inner authority to act on their own.

The franchise "authorization" for many is worth the whole fee. People join unions and professional associations for similar reasons, even when joining is voluntary.

The Power of Permission reaches deeply into all our lives. Even powerful, mature men have found they needed "permission"—release from nameless guilt—when they saw themselves, quite without having planned it that way, living longer on this earth than their own fathers. literally, such men need permission if they are to live longer than dear old dad without feeling miserable about it. If dad was permission giver and model for their lives, they may need professional help to feel comfortable outliving him.

The same need for permission to live is seen in those cases where a husband or wife barely outlives a departed spouse. We say they died of a broken heart, having nothing left to live for. But is it possible the survivor no longer felt inner authorization to stay alive? Did permission to live expire with the one they loved?

Permission by Example

Permission by example is frequent also, as when someone becomes a physician or lawyer or firefighter or teacher because it is family tradition. For example, if your family name is Kennedy, you may have more permission than the next fellow to run for president.

Sometimes the example that frees is the colleague at work or the person next door who successfully launches an unexpected new career. Sometimes the example is the boss himself, the employee looking frankly at the person in charge and deciding, "If he can do it, I certainly can do it just as well or better."

Alexander the Great, whom we might consider the one person in history who would not need permission to conquer the world, is yet a prime example of one who desperately sought authorization for his bold conquests every time he subdued a new nation. His biographers have long puzzled over why, in every possible case, he sought out the oracles of any great religious shrines in lands he conquered, each time coming out of the temple—after disappearing inside for hours or days— to proclaim himself the truly begotten son of that particular god or goddess.

It did two things for him. First, it was a convincing demonstration to the beaten peoples that he would respect their religion and way of life; it in fact cloaked him in the power and authority of their belief, making them easier to rule than if he had burned down their temples.

Second, it apparently gave him the "permission" his soul required to do as his teacher Aristotle had taught him (be a philosopher-king), permission his competitive father, Philip of Macedon, must have refused him.

Even mighty Napoleon felt need for higher "authority" when he had himself crowned Emperor in a cathedral, though he snatched the crown from the Pope's hand and placed it on his head himself.

Sickness as Permission

Permission can come disguised in unexpected forms, such as illness. An illness offers permission to sit on the sidelines awhile, avoiding decisions and conflicts, while receiving the special privileges accorded the ill. When reentering the world at large later on, it is often with a new "contract" or understanding of what one will accept from the world.

Many alive today owe their longer lifespan to the work of a sickly-seeming spinster from England. Florence Nightingale almost single-handedly revolutionized hospital standards, sanitation, patient care, and the education of nurses in the last century. She converted hospitals from houses of death to places of hope. Yet she spent most of her adult life abed, chained there by ill-defined illness, in the romantic manner favored by Victorians.

She left her frequent bed at thirty-four for the battlefields of the Crimean War where British soldiers were dying unnecessarily, due to the poor standards of medical care at the time. After remarkable exploits, saving lives in her model hospitals with her corps of trained nurses, she returned home to England—to a perpetual sickbed, from which she somehow managed to found, at forty, the Nightingale School and Home for nurses in London. Her biographers claim her health was broken by her labors, but she managed to survive and work another half-century, expiring at last at ninety! She never left the shade of her home again after the Crimea. But the world of the powerful and the famous beat a path to her bedside, from which she continued the medical revolution she had begun.

Poor Florence Nightingale did not have permission to lead a conventional life, to marry, to raise a family or even stand on her own two feet much of the time. But she did have permission to be "sick"—an honorable occupation for Victorian females. Since few other occupations were open to women at the time, somehow her "sickness" permitted her to work toward the healing of others.

As a source of permission or release, sickness is rather weak but widely resorted to, known even in jokes. It is a staple of theater, the "sick" mother whose threatened heart attacks give her power to command her grown children, who obey her strident voice because no one (other than a physician) has authority to deny a dying woman her wish.

The healthier form of problem avoidance is the vacation, retreat, or sabbatical away from daily cares. Positive changes in living grow out of these formal rest times more often than from sick time, but both are means of escaping from problems long enough to get permission to look at life a new way.

Conversion as Permission

Permission to follow a higher path often comes from religious conversion experiences. One of the best known examples in our culture is that of Saint Paul in the New Testament. Saul (as he was known before his shattering conversion on the road to Damascus) was a credentialist of the first magnitude, carrying documents from the highest religious authorities of his time, allowing him to ferret out heretics for trial. After a two-year hiatus at the "backside of the desert" Paul asserted his divine authority—received in a blinding light and a voice no one else could hear on the Damascus Road—to become the first official Christian missionary to Europe and the West.

The Group as Permission Giver

Permission, not always of the positive sort, may be given by one's group, gang, or peers. Ask any grade school teacher or juvenile officer. Its manifestations in the adult world are "company policy" and local tradition.

If you think about it, the Soviet political system is based on the local group as permission giver to the individual. How else do you interpret the revolutionary slogan "All power to the Soviets" (the workers' councils)? Unlike the American system where power comes from "the people," in Russia, it ostensibly comes from "councils" or Soviets of the people. Quite a different thing, and one capable of exerting much control over individual members who need the group's consent in order to live.

We are wise to consider "permission from the peer group" not so much permission as a disguised form of authority one is expected to obey.

Permission to Be Positive

The reason for this exploration of how humans hunger for permission to live their lives fully has to do with the fact that without permission to lift their heads higher, none can hope to make their way up the Positive-Power Pyramid. Lacking authority to dream, to act, to change, to be different, to win, they have all the permission in the world NOT to dream, NOT to act, NOT to change, NOT to be different, and NOT to win.

How, then, do we find our necessary authority to begin? Some fortunate few find it very young in life, so early it seems always to have existed as an inner reality for them. They exude this inner authority—a seemingly self-generated permission to do things—and the world says they have charisma and follows them.

Where does that leave the rest of us, who have to work hard at whatever it is we achieve in life? How do we find ourselves passports to leave the old life behind?

It helps to understand that the reason more people have not made the Positive Thinker's life their own is that no one told them they could. So who's to tell them? Most likely they must tell themselves. That's the still, small voice they are hearing, when people say "something told me I could."

In a permissive society such as ours, one would think getting permission to do good things—especially the right thing for oneself—would be the easiest thing imaginable. But since it is not, then let us find our authority where we must, so we can progress to the next simple step in our quest for the secret of Positive Thinkers' success.

Start by asking yourself, what stands in the way of your upward reach? If you get answers like "I don't think I can do it" or "No one in our family has ever gone that far," you do have a permission problem.

It's one thing to say "I don't know HOW I can do it" and quite another to assert "I don't think I CAN do it." Ignorance can yield to knowledge but disbelief in oneself needs to be dispelled by authoritative permission.

Often the best way to gain this permission is to get all the education it takes to qualify in your field. The danger for some is that education will become a life delaying end in itself that lasts a lifetime.

One way of getting permission is to start out anyway, just as if you had a license from God or someone, admitting you don't really have authority if someone should challenge you. Then go as far as you can—and see if anyone does challenge you. Few ever will. They have permission worries of their own, no doubt. After a certain point you will find that your own hesitating success is ail the authority you need to continue the rest of the way.

Success breeds success... and authority for even more.

Often, it is the belief that another has in you that gives you all the permission or authority you can possibly use in a lifetime. A believing friend, spouse, or parent can be enough to sustain you through times of self-doubt. It is worth remarking that many great leaders of history had extraordinarily strong relationships with totally supportive mothers. Julius Caesar, Franklin D. Roosevelt, Genera! Douglas MacArthur, and Abraham Lincoln (encouraged by his stepmother Nancy Hanks) come immediately to mind. Whatever else we may think about these men, there is little question they had an early inner permission to succeed.

The simple words "I believe in you" may be all the permission you need to achieve happiness and success.

If all else fails, consider the uses of adversity. It's a storybook staple, how the inventor, entrepreneur, or composer, down to his last dollar in cash and deeply in debt, succeeds at the last moment because he cannot afford to fail. I do not recommend eyeball-depth debt, but sometimes the best use you can make of an overwhelming problem is to let it give you permission to do what you might never dare attempt otherwise.

Finally, if you find yourself in surroundings where the endorsement of others is not feasible, a truly effective way to give oneself the inner permission to set goals and climb the Positive-Power Pyramid is this ritual: Write yourself a formal memorandum, which you keep, that says:

I believe I have the right and the duty to grow and reach beyond my present circumstances.

Date it, sign it, and keep a copy with you at all times during the next several days to read and reread.

What we see in writing is easier to believe. You will soon find out whether you are in the 5 percent or 95 percent crowd by how your mind reacts to this assertion of your freedom to grow.

If you find an otherwise unexplainable enthusiasm creeping into your thoughts and feel a growing eagerness to get on to better things, you will know you have crossed the Permission barrier, if you have not already.

Pyramids are broadest at the base and get smaller each step upward. "Positive Permission" is the base of our Pyramid and obviously more people flunk out at this level than anywhere else. They don't climb higher because they lack inner permission to do so. We've looked at why this is true and some ways this lack can be overcome.

Now it is time to see what we are being given authority to do.

Posi/Thoughts

Permission for success can come from many sources—ceremony, outside authority, example, time for reflection, a spiritual experience or a social group. All these external grants of permission, however, merely echo the inner permission to achieve with which we are born.

GOALS
Are the
DNA
Of the Soul

CHAPTER SIX

STEP TWO
Positive Goal-Setting:
The True Limits of Achievement

hree things mark the difference between mature humans and alt the rest of God's creatures:

- We are aware that we shall someday not be here; we shall die.
- We possess the gift of laughter; no other being can laugh... or needs to.
- We are able to change the future (not merely our own destiny) by our setting of long-range goals, toward which to strive.

Philosophers have long ruminated, remarked, and written on the first two points, our mortality and our frivolity. Few, if any, have dwelt on the third. Most people seem totally blind to our race's greatest gift, our ability to select alternative tomorrows, to remake our world to accord with our dreams.

If it's allowed for at all, the most serious expression it may get is to pop up in one of those wistful songs of the musical stage where the unlikely hero or heroine emits a solo against an unbelieving world, telling it what they wish the world were like, and what they want to do about it.

That's why people love to sing about climbing every mountain, fording every stream, looking for bluebirds of happiness, and flying somewhere over the rainbow. The only place they think it's legal to pursue great goals is in the dream world of the stage, far from real life. And that's not so.

What a bitter, hateful God created us IF, in denying us the merciful ignorance of death accorded the rest of His organic world, the only compensation He gave us were... LAUGHTER! Life would be a joke. And the joke would be on

God's compensation to us for knowing so much about our inevitable future—and even there He offers an attractive alternative—is to give us the power to make of our days what we will, and make over the world to our own ideals. We do this through the establishment of our true goals in life.

Goals are symbols that speak of very real things, the real things we shall one day have, achieve, or be if we're successful. One definition *I* use is this: *Goals are coordinates in time and space which you plan to visit in the future.*

When you set a goal for yourself, you are really making an appointment with yourself to have certain pleasant things happen at a certain future place and time, as the result of coordinated actions you take between now and then.

This sets goals in perspective, removing them from the realm of wish-magic. Goals can only be played out in the four dimensional arena of time (our lifespan) and space (our world).

We are beings with the strange gift of being able to affect what WILL BE in the future, by our choices, based on our inner goals. This great gift is wasted if it is used merely to nod yes or no to whatever thin soup of a choice life serves up on a given day.

At critical times, life gives us a blunt choice: *Goals or controls.*

If we fail to establish goals, we shall have no choice but to serve and be controlled by those who do set goals for themselves, for in time the world will configure itself to their purposes, not ours. We end up being bit players on life's stage, when we could have been directors, playwrights, or stars.

By our setting of goals, we vote for our tomorrows. If you don't vote, you can't complain about how things get run.

Many view life as a kind of game, and in some ways it is. Not because some win and some lose, but because games have time limits. That, life certainly does. Our timer gives us maybe 28,000 days in which to win, lose... or draw back.

What we win or lose or run away from is whatever stake we play for in those seventy-five years or so. Our "stake" is another name for life goals, which we have about 660,000 hours to reach, starting with our first breath.

We are born optimists. Else why do babies smile? As infants we truly believe the world is there to please and satisfy us. If we were not native optimists—anticipating overall favorable results from whatever comes our way—we could not survive. The real nonoptimist is the suicide.

Our inborn optimism is great stuff. But it is not enough to build a life on. It is no substitute for proper goals to strive for. We live with a desperate hunger for goals, which most societies of the past routinely provided for their people. Ours does not.

If we turn off the noise around us and listen, we hear muffled inner voices, like echoes in a seashell, telling of our need to be part of something greater than ourselves. If we do not fall into that "something greater" early, by accident, or by some institution's design on us (i.e., an evangelizing church, a radical political party) we struggle to find something to fill the void.

When we say we are looking for the meaning of life, we are really saying we lack a goal that satisfies us. We yearn to identify with something greater than ourselves. That is all that a worthy goal is.

Borrowed Coals

Like picking up the wrong coat in a restaurant, it is sometimes possible to go a long way cloaked in another person's goals. Parents sometimes pin accidental goals on a child by repeatedly letting the child overhear them describing him to others as possessing a certain destiny. The problem occurs when the youngster takes the parental fantasy for a life command. "Our eldest boy is the bright one. He's going to be a lawyer or a doctor for sure." What if he would rather be a potter instead? Rebellion may be the only way out of his bind. Or organized failure.

The "stage child" is a frequent victim of borrowed or transferred star struck goals—the parents' own, usually, since the child cannot legally sign its own contracts.

Ambassador Joseph Kennedy, himself at one time strongly involved in Hollywood film production, set "stage child" goals for his eldest son and namesake. He assigned him the role of becoming a national political star. With the loss of that son in war, the goal was reassigned by the family to brother John F. Kennedy, then by the news media at later dates to brothers Robert and Teddy in their turn.

One may wonder if any of the Kennedy males were ever consulted about these goals or if they had them so early imprinted on the soul as to make the question moot.

The Kennedy clan *Camelot* script which the ambassador wrote for his sons, passed between them like an heirloom. Perversely, it was to play itself out like one of those strange stories from Ripley's "Believe It Or Not!" One is never sure the event really happened, yet the Ripley story holds a horrid fascination:

The brothers in a poor family mysteriously fall ill and die, each in his turn, starting with the eldest, following the death of their father from a rattlesnake bite.

As each brother assumes the role of eldest surviving male, he inherits *his father's prized boots, the only item of value left to the survivors. Only after several of the sons have died does anyone examine the inherited boots, which the father was wearing the day he died.*

Embedded deep in the leather, unnoticed, are found broken-off rattler fangs. The hidden hypodermics had scratched each brother in turn when he tried on his elder's inheritance. The fangs retained enough dried venom to sicken and slowly kill them all, when they tried to stand in their father's shoes.

Empty Goals

If borrowed goals sometimes work, they can lead, as the Kennedy clan saga shows, to disaster as well. The same is true of empty goals.

Empty goals are frequently chosen because friends and relatives say they are the right ones to have. Many women, not to speak of their surprised mates and ill-prepared children, suffered pathetic damage in the late sexual revolution because they accepted, unthinkingly, the goals of radical female thinkers, then darlings of the media, who outspokenly denounced, decried, and despised the "empty" goals of their own mothers... and got a generation of media-influenced women to trade them in for flashier, yet equally empty ones.

If it was wrong for one generation to teach its young women that the only satisfaction in life and hope for their full employment was matrimony and motherhood, it was no less wrong—perhaps worse, for the children involved—for another generation to insist that the only true female happiness to be found on planet Earth was behind a desk, counter, or machine.

The Russians put all their women into the paid workforce because so many men had been killed off by war. The Americans tricked theirs into the workforce by killing off their marriages. The word "tricked" is the right one. It emphasizes the bitterness felt by any reflective person who ever pursued a goal society seemed to insist on—only to find it hollow, once bitten into. The anger is the same, whether these empty goals are mandatory matrimony, Victorian style, or salary slavery, today's style. Only the victims are different.

Why be a victim? If you adopt goals that you have not really examined, modified, or made your own, you stand a fair chance of being a victim, not a victor.

Misleading Goals

Sometimes we will choose goals for ourselves that have two possible outcomes: The advertised good one and an unmentioned bad one we'll likely pull down on our heads because we didn't know two outcomes were bundled as one seemingly safe goal.

For instance, how many people have failed at college because their official goal was to get a degree... but the real purpose of attending college was to get their folks off their backs?

Once in the academic environment many students will fall into the spirit of the thing and trudge on through, somehow. But a goodly number will drop out because their script only called for college, not career or success. Having stopped the mouths of their parents with finality, they are now free to drift on to other things.

The mutually accepted goal (college) had one meaning to them, another to their parents.

How many babies will never live to hear a mother's lullaby because one of its parents misleads the other about the goal of their love?

Our culture does not help much, promoting widespread confusion about love. Broken homes are a poor place for children to learn fuller understanding of this basic goal of life. Too few women anymore—or men—can distinguish between love with commitment and love in general. Just so it feels good while it lasts, seems the idea.

Most misleading goals can be recognized and avoided by asking one question. *"Am I seeking this for myself? Or am I saying I want this mostly to placate someone else?"*

There is nothing wrong in choosing goals that please other people. But you have your own life to lead first. And you do not always get multiple occasions to start over with blank paper. That's why it is so important to make the most of your goals and choose them carefully. You just might get what you ask for.

Default Goals

Nature abhors a vacuum. If it's empty, she'll fill it. If you do not erect sturdy goals of your own, a whole raft of "default goals" will fill the vacant spot in your soul. Who knows where they will come from? You certainly won't.

Goals are idealistic statements. Yet some terribly destructive ideologies (e.g., Marxism) express themselves in terms of attractive sounding, idealistic goals. One can easily fill the mind with scoops of contaminated goals that look good and seem right but are self-destructive, or, like Marxism, demand the deaths of millions of human beings if they are to come true.

Better to have no goals than to live for those acquired without thinking, especially if they require others to suffer.

Default goals are like deadly disease virus particles that invade a living cell and commandeer its mechanisms to make copies of itself to invade and destroy other cells. By surrendering, without thought, to default goals, one surrenders the whole purpose of life. Instead of your life counting for good, it might count for the wrong.

Of goals, good and bad, it can truly be said "Goals *are the DNA of the soul.*" Bad DNA, bad genes, bad goals, are destructive to life. Good DNA, good genes, good goals enhance life... ARE life.

Goals preserve the soul and dreams of mankind as truly as double-helix DNA molecules preserve the genetic code of our bodies, defining our form, appearance, traits, and lifespans.

Our physical selves are transmitted in coded form to the long future by packets of DNA in our genes, to reappear again in new form. Our ideal selves (our goal selves) are forwarded to the future encoded in the "spiritual DNA" we call goals, which are our long-term ideals.

If puzzled as to what your life goals should be, ask yourself, what are your long-term ideals? What do you deeply believe in? Your goals will usually be found in that neighborhood somewhere, waiting for you to recognize them.

If you seem to lack goals, many institutions carry large inventories of plausible "default goals" in a wide range of sizes ready to hang on you, unless you put up fierce resistance and insist you already have your own, thank you.

Be wary of predatory institutions that keep their best people in underpaid servitude by offering up default goals that exploit the natural desire for a decent lot in life. These stated goals are mostly a ploy to get more work out of undergoaled, underpaid underlings.

Of course, the "future executive" is told, climbing to that elevated status requires certain extra sacrifices like longer hours, no incentive pay, higher sales targets, etc., while proving one's mettle.

The hopeful employee, usually young, is offered a carrot for a goal, and that promised for delivery in the sweet by and by. It often causes someone to spend extra years at the bottom of the ladder, with no special gain. To someone with unasserted goals, the experience can be life wasting and a distraction from getting started on what is really important to them.

If you do not assert your goals, institutions invariably will assert theirs for you, frequently to your detriment. At best, you'll be swept along in their slipstream. At worst, your personal goals will fall under their wheels, lucky not to be ground to bits.

Not all institutions are so malignant, but some are, so it pays to be wary. Institutions are said to be the lengthened shadow of their founders. These are usually people of strong resolve, high dreams, and tall goals. It is hard to compete with such people, even when they are dead.

Happily, there are some benign institutions whose goals may converge with your own and pull you higher than you at first dared to dream. Among these are good schools, certain kinds of churches, and forward-looking businesses. If you can find an institutional "goal mate," by all means do, if that is what you truly want.

Shared Goals

On the "soul mate" side of life, your personal goals are as important as those on the job. To share meals, bed, and dwelling with someone whose goals do not encompass your own is to share deep pain as well.

How often have you seen married couples live in apparent compatibility until one member becomes aware of a compelling inner goal, and is driven to reach it? The stress on their marriage can be as severe as infidelity. The noninspired member, in fact, may come to view pursuit of the newly expressed goal by their otherwise partner as a kind of adultery, something that breaks their banding.

Shared lives walk a shared path wending toward shared goals. *"Can two walk together, except they be agreed?"* asks the Bible.

The assumption of shared goal stands behind every marriage ceremony, but is often mistaken. Some marriage partners are better at accepting the "for worse" part of the marriage vow than the "for better." If things go badly, if the couple fails to prosper economically, they find a way to cope.

But if things go extremely well, if the goal-directed member creates sudden new wealth, the other partner may not be able to deal with the consequences of the unexpected abundance and may begin displaying bizarre behavior.

Spendthrift spouses and marriage partners who labor assiduously at alienating children from the goal-driven parent, are examples of this behavior. Alcoholism is another. And sometimes it may coil back and strike the more successful partner because he or she feels so utterly abandoned by the one they trusted.

Hollywood marriages frequently turn out as they do because there are no shared goals other than to gratify the celebrity gossip media. The couples recycle readily because one marriage can be good for several blasts of media attention: courtship, ceremony, honeymoon, first problems, breakup and divorce, play boy/play girl phase.

Yet many marriages do survive the late development of strong goals in the life of one partner. The dedication page of almost any book you pick up expresses the gratitude of the author for the spouse's tolerance of the writer's need to complete the manuscript. Many women marry a man with a solid career ahead as broker, banker, salesman, or teacher, only to have him throw it all over when undergoing a mid-career crisis. Yet they will stay with him if he elects to become an inn operator in New Hampshire or a missionary to Borneo or a franchise operator in Florida. Call it love or call it shared goals. Maybe it's the same thing.

In a more primitive time, when sheer survival was a sufficient goal for most families, other shared goals were not as important, as people died younger and did not all live to an age to see their dreams come true.

As recently as 100 years ago some sturdy specimens might bury several spouses, without having to have much regard to their short-lived dreams. The survivor might achieve long-term goals because each spouse contributed labor, dowry, or inheritance to help him or her along.

Today, odds are both parties to a marriage will live a very long time. It behooves them to have shared goals worth working happily toward together over the years.

Goal Substitutes

Can anything take the place of true goals in life? Perhaps not, for they seem to be demanded by the structures of human minds, helping us to live purposefully. (Something we crave to the point of believing the impossible.)

Optimism is sometimes tried as a substitute for the reality of a good substantial goal to tie one's life to. But it does not endure, for optimism is forced to believe that something better is always near at hand (never necessarily arriving, of course) but near enough to wait for.

And it is the waiting that erodes the value of empty optimism. A person with a real goal to achieve might pack accomplishment of some kind into the wasted wait period, working closer to his goals, while another trusts optimism.

Optimism's unsmiling sister, Fate, is an even more dangerous stand-in for worthy goals. She plays for higher stakes. Unlike optimism, which promises a better tomorrow, fate promises nothing at all, and may take everything you own and did not understand that you were risking.

The Secret Advantage Goal-Setters Enjoy

Fate, chance, random events, cannot replace the goals we require to live as creatures made in the image of God. For if one is to trust fate for every good thing in life, it is worth remembering that fate always guarantees more losers than winners in any lottery. If you trust fate, you have one chance in millions. If you trust your goals, you have every chance in the world.

Fate, chance, and random events dictate to most people, but to the Positive Thinker/Achiever with strong goals, they become serendipitous circumstances. Chance encounters that might only be empty experiences to the drifting soul without clear goals, become platinum-plated possibilities to the one with Positive Goals.

Napoleon Hill first brought this to my understanding in his most famous book, *Think and Grow Rich.* He showed that the purpose-filled individual (primed with goals) so activated unused parts of his subconscious mind to achieve his goals, that something worthwhile was obtained from almost every chance encounter in that person's life. Entering a room full of strangers, the goal-enriched person has the advantage over everyone there. Every stray bit of knowledge to be picked up in the room somehow adheres to him, fueling new insights into solving the problems that will achieve the driving goals.

Positive Thinkers' Goals

It has been necessary to this point to consider some hazards that can accompany goal setting. Not all goals, as we've seen, are good—or even good for you.

Understanding that, let us consider a few rules that will help you, as Positive Thinker/Achiever, sort out your own goals for your own unique life. They are part of the Secret of Positive Thinkers' Success.

Positive Thinkers' Goals are always

- *Measurable.*
- *Life-enhancing.*
- *As specific as possible.*

Positive Thinkers' Goals differ from the generalized background goals picked up at home and school, which are fuzzy in focus and more like good intentions than purposeful planning aids. Background goals are less a product of our inspired will and more like the biases of our character.

For example, it is common to assert as a life goal the desire to have a peaceful, happy home life. Is that a true Positive Thinkers' Goal? Not really. It is life-enhancing, yes. And somewhat specific (peaceful, happy) but it cannot be measured, so it does not meet the full three-part test.

Positive Thinkers' Goals are meant to be attained, so they must be measurable in some objective manner An unbiased outsider, must be able to recognize that you have obtained your goal, that it is not simply some subjective, somatic feeling you attain after a lot of hard work. It is not a self-triggered sensation of nirvana that tells you it is all right to quit striving.

You MUST be able to tell when goals have been achieved. Goals, as we mean them, are not the same as purpose in life. One's purpose or desire, let us say, may be to become a benefactor of the human race. There are a thousand ways to do this. Only a few will normally be within any single person's ability or lifespan to achieve, no matter how inspired.

One may fulfill an underlying high purpose (benefactor of mankind) by developing a cure for cancer. Or by making a (measurable) billion dollars to fund a foundation that helps the Third World hungry to feed themselves. Or by teaching one child.

The goal is measurable even if the unit is ONE. But it must be measurable.

Positive Thinkers' Goals must also be life-enhancing, as I said. This stipulation is more readily understandable than the one on measurable goals to most people, it is bound up in the nature of life itself: Abundance!

Life is prolific. Life multiplies. Life grows. It fills every life-tolerant cranny of our planet and would overclimb the universe likewise if given the chance. Positive Thinker/ Achievers position themselves always on the side of life, because that is where God has placed Himself. Else they risk using the gift for death, including their own.

We serve a God of abundance in a world and universe of abundance. Our trees are not born with one or two leaves, but hundreds of thousands. Abundance! Our forests are not made of one or two specimen trees, but millions. More abundance! Our oceans teem with life. Our land surfaces too, with life forms we can see, and more we cannot see.

We know that people are not born with just one or two options for achievement in life, but an abundance of them. (If you did not inwardly believe that, you would not be reading this book.)

Life produces. And those who produce the most, the 5 percenters again, perhaps live the most.

The requirement that proper Positive Thinkers' Goals must be as specific as possible is what makes true goal setting more than a casual rite. It takes deep thought and a certain amount of living to do. If anyone below puberty sets a strong life goal which is ultimately realized, it is usually the result of a trauma that forced the goal maker to face the reality of life very early.

Many decisions to enter medicine are made at a tender age, it is reported, usually as the result of a youngster experiencing the death of a close relative. The angry child asserts it will fight death by becoming a physician. And the eventual adult complies, studies hard, wins a degree, and opens a practice.

However, if no further goals have been set since the triggering trauma in childhood, society can be left with a dangerously bored doctor whose golf game and investments are all he lives for, other than the thrill of cheating death.

Goals help us shape what we become. We must choose them carefully. And when we reach them, it is best to have others to reach for in reserve. For we are not done growing until we leave this world.

For all of us, and the Positive Thinker/Achiever especially, goals are vital. Coals are only symbols, we know. But they are symbols with payoffs, every one.

Posi/Thoughts

We choose our tomorrows by the goals we select.

These goals must be our own or truly made our own, not borrowed, not devoid of purpose, not misleading in direction or imposed by some powerful ideology without thought on our part.

Optimism without goals or effort is useless and self-destructive.

Positive Thinkers seek goals that are measurable, life-enhancing and as specific as possible.

*Change the
Polarity
Of Your
Thinking and
Everything Else
Changes Too*

CHAPTER SEVEN

STEP THREE
Positive Goal-Picturing
What You "See" Is What You Get

In caves near Altamira, Spain, an astonishing array of strange wall drawings was discovered deep inside the earth in 1879. They soon became the focus of controversy and mystery. Their origin could not be explained by either the science or the religion of the time, due to the unexpected subjects portrayed in the sketches and the skill with which they were

The puzzling paintings depicted with bold, masterly strokes strange prehistoric animals of a kind no human had seen in the flesh for more than 15,000 years. Whoever had so skillfully painted these extinct animals clearly did it from experience, not imagination, and must have seen the creatures often enough in the bright outside world to reproduce them in vivid detail far inside a dark, sunless cave by torchlight.

While the debate raged, other caves in northern Spain and southern France started to yield similar treasures of prehistoric art. Most remarkable were drawings discovered in Lascaux, France, in 1942. By this time a consensus had been reached: the art—whatever its exact meaning—was probably the product of Cro-Magnon hunters who visited the deep recesses of these caves for the specific purpose of making these visualizations of things important to them in their now long forgotten world.

Many today feel these remote inner caves and their art comprised the Ice Age equivalent of a cathedral or "holy of holies," a center for secret religious ritual screened away from the profane eyes of the world. If so, it would seem that primitive cave men could draw well enough to command our respect even today, and had developed this high human skill in response to a specific need.

What was that need? Perhaps the very one we are discussing, the need to make clear pictures of our most intensely sought goals, to hold them clearly in mind to pursue and win.

Unlike wall drawings found in many of the full-fledged civilizations that followed, the cave pictures of Lascaux do not seem to be a history—a record of something that really happened at a certain time and place. Rather, they appear to be what we might call wish-pictures, symbols of the hopes and goals of the imaginative people who made them.

Where you and I might use imagination (and a handy yellow legal pad) for the purpose of visualizing the goals that motivate us, the skin-clad hunters of this early Ice Age culture found it useful to make precise drawings of the objects of their desire: fat, healthy bison for meat and hide; fleet, pregnant deer whose bellies promised more good hunting next season.

To these earliest goal-picturing ancestors of ours the animals sketched represented their goals and hopes for the future— food, clothing, and some surplus to let them enjoy a few days respite from the relentless pressure of survival.

I ask, what do we picture for ourselves today that is so very different?

It is interesting and exciting for us to see that among these early relics of human culture we should find evidence of selected goals being pictured—visualized before their achievement—in a manner that others could share.

This goal picturing is something we are good at, as human beings. So good in fact, we often overdo it and waste our visualizing powers on our worries, not our goals. Since our subconscious minds work eagerly and constantly to help us achieve whatever goals we fill our minds with, you can see why worrisome people tend to bring upon themselves the very calamities they fear.

Without intending, they treat their fears like goals... and receive in real life the feared, negative things their minds are filled with. Which should not surprise them.

They have grabbed the gun by the barrel, not the stock, and shot themselves in the foot.

So strong is our inborn ability to visualize what is not present before our eyes, we are the only creature on earth that has to be reminded, "Live for today. Stop to smell the flowers. Take time to live now, for tomorrow never gets here." Images of what we see coming at us (rightly or wrongly) can block out what is apparent in front of us. Our ability to picture things that MAY come to pass can keep us from observing those that HAVE come to pass. Improperly focused wish-pictures can overpower the senses and keep reality from registering on our behavior.

The good side to this innate trait is that with thought and practice you can channel its power into picturing your most strongly desired goals and help them become substantial realities the rest of the world must deal with. To this extent, at least, we are born with ability to determine our destiny and to alter the course of everything around us by the goals we picture into existence and leave behind us.

Society's "Picture" Frames

Since all human groupings, from civilizations and religions to yacht clubs and hunting parties, are based on shared goals, it is not surprising that we are familiar with large numbers of the shared images that help groups pursue those goals.

Christians are pretty well agreed about heaven as a goal, for example, and it is widely sung about in the older hymns. How much poorer the world of art would be without the great cathedrals, paintings, sculptures, and carvings designed to convey some aspect or image of heaven as a place for the saints to dwell in the eternal presence of God.

Yet many of the once commonly shared images of Christendom have lost their power because they have lost meaning. To think of God as King of Heaven was potent imagery for all the many centuries before the rise of the large industrial democracies and dictatorships. Now kings rarely hold real power (the few that remain). The images they conjure in the mind are of playboys, signs on hamburger stands, the first name of a monster movie gorilla, or a suitable name for an aggressive dog.

We are left with the shell of an image, one unable to evoke strong loyalty or strong desire. This problem of powerless imagery baffles many old-line institutions in our day. Undermined by rapid changes in the meaning of the symbols that describe and locate them, their potential followers do not know where to find them or understand what they do.

What we are seeing is the decline of once powerful institutions because of a failure of their imagery—their mind pictures about themselves—to keep up with change. In this is a great lesson for us about the tremendous power of those symbols we choose to store in our minds. When we operate under the right ones (for us) we are nearly unstoppable. When the wrong mind-pictures dominate us, we can't get started.

Cults, corporations, revolutionaries, sports teams, nations. Scout troops, all operate under implicitly agreed on sets of mental pictures of what the world really is or should be. That's why so many such entities demand pledges or commitments or vows from those who join, to work toward these common ideals.

If a goal cannot be expressed in clear, attractive, and meaningful images, it has no future. This is true whether the goal is to find the Holy Grail or blaze an explorer's rocket trail to the planets.

Your own future is directly linked to the images and goal-pictures you maintain in your mind. At this very moment you are WHO you are and WHERE you are because of what you've allowed to inhabit your goal-box. The Bible says it this way (Proverbs 23:7), *"As he thinketh in his heart, so is he."*

Interfering Images

Jehovah knew what He was doing when He commanded the Israelites not to make graven images. The power of mental imagery to dominate behavior is so strong that to reinforce it with visual imagery as well—a well-carved erotic statue of some debauched Philistine deity, say—could make a false god seem so real as to undo the entire contract (covenant) the invisible Jehovah had struck with Moses and Abraham.

Better that the God with an inexpressible name should have an unexpressed countenance as well.

While we moderns are not much tempted to fall on our knees before statues of golden calves (a frequent failing of the Israelites), our culture has its own failing for mental images that interfere with the goals we profess. These interfering images stray some victims into meaningless pursuits and immobilize others for years or lifetimes.

These much sought after but unusable mind-pictures lack an ultimate grounding in any outer reality, being mostly the random electrical output of brains under the influence of recreational drugs. The trouble is, these spurious signals take up just as much mind-space and productive life as benign imagery. Minds teeming with untamed, drug-assisted images tend to achieve little in life except to shorten it. And those who extract some meaning from their chemical kaleidoscopy and consciously try to reach its elusive goal sometimes find it under the name of Insanity.

False images that interfere with our goal-picturing ability may include such things as the wrong kind of daydreams. Properly used, daydreams can be a powerful aid to remaking your world to conform with your goals, for they offer a remote inner cave of the mind for prime visual rehearsals of the goals you wish to obtain.

However, almost by definition, most daydreams do not lead to productive activity; they are an escape from it. They commonly serve as low investment wish fulfillers, substitutes for actually doing something. That is not to say daydreams cannot be rechanneled into serving your vital need for "seeing" the future fruit of your dreams, and so energize your subconscious mind into finding ways to get it.

At the least, constructive daydreams may serve like the personal pictures soldiers carry in their battle gear to remind them what they are fighting for.

Displacing Bad Imagery

A normal mind is like an overpriced hotel. Reputation demands that every room be considered occupied or reserved, whether it really is or not. You may walk up to the desk and ask for a room, and not get one, though the place is near empty. The brain-hotel likes to think of itself as busy with important matters at all times, loaded to legal limits and with a waiting list to attend to, perhaps when life is a little less clamorous.

This is, of course, not true. Most of the chambers remain empty. Only the elevators are busy.

That means there's plenty of room for new ideas, new ways of winning riches and solving problems, once you get past the self-importance of the front desk and onto the automatic elevator of imagery that connects all floors of the mind.

This may call for some "image displacement." It's a very old concept, spoken of in the Bible, where Saint Paul admonishes "whatever things are true... honest... just... pure... lovely... of good report... THINK ON THESE THINGS." In another place he quotes Jesus as saying "overcome evil with good." That is, displace the bad with the good.

You must grab the elevator and displace its loitering load of trivia and stifling negation with positive pictures of the goals you strongly desire to achieve. Only then will you control what takes lodging in your brain, which is a matter of profound importance to you. For whatever occupies the mind tends to produce physical results both in you and in the world outside.

That is why Norman Vincent Peak's teaching— "Change *your thinking and you change everything*"—has been so effective with millions. Strong mental pictures of our goals are as redeemable for reality as a check is for cash. Our visualized goals have payoffs in our attitudes, our behavior, our expectations, our efforts, our achievements.

This is true for negative images as well.

The old, negative, and bad for us images that we've practiced for a lifetime can die hard. Old learning (even when wrong) tends to override new learning (even the best), until the new is overlearned and made habitual.

If you ever lacked evidence of this, think back to some stressful time when you had to pass a driving test for a license or a swimming test for a grade. If you panicked for any reason-—getting a demon examiner for your road test, or being shoved off the diving board when you did not expect it—you automatically reverted to earlier, more heavily practiced, behavior patterns. You momentarily forgot how to drive or swim and could easily have hit a tree or drowned. Your newer learning was undone by the old, which you had practiced so much longer.

Beware your investment in old images that keep you from going where you want with your life, toward the new goals you are positively imaging, picturing into reality.

Yours would not be the first case where an investment in old images—literally—held back human progress and, in one instance, the exploration of the world. It happened in the centuries following Columbus that each new decade brought vast new geographical discoveries and a more exact knowledge of the shape of the land masses of the world.

There was a market for this information in the form of printed aliases containing maps of the discoveries and other navigational data. Cartographers, as mapmakers call themselves, could easily reset and reprint pages of relatively inexpensive movable type as new facts became known. But their investment was much heavier in the laboriously hand-engraved metal plates from which maps were printed, so they hesitated to replace them any of tener than forced to by their competitors.

As a result, serious navigational errors wasted lives and resources unnecessarily because sailors' maps did not reflect the latest knowledge of coastlines, harbors, shoals, and currents. For scores of years expeditions languished, fleets failed to return to port, armies died. All because a handful of European cartographers felt they had too great an investment in old printing plates—old images—to offer corrected, updated maps to the seafaring public!

Exploration itself was held back. Even the old Latin phrase that adorned vacant corners of the unaltered maps *(ne plus ultra)* was taken to mean "Nothing EXISTS beyond this point," subtly discouraging exploration. Had the phrase been reinforced with new maps, it might have been construed more properly as "Nothing is KNOWN beyond this point," a permission-giving challenge to new exploration.

We must be willing to invest in new images of the goals we hope to achieve, discarding the old by displacing them with the new.

Don't actively try to kill off old ideas. You'll be foiled by the mind's "Hippopotamus Response." (Spend the next five minutes NOT thinking of the word "hippopotamus." It's almost impossible to do, of course.) You cannot think of the things you want thrown out of your head without PICTURING them... and making them stronger. Only displacement works. Displace old ideas with the pictured goals you want your mind to pursue with the same persistence that it repaints "hippopotamus" in your brain each time you tell it to forget.

Burning in New Goal Pictures

Prior to their prowess in manufacturing electronic devices and automobiles, the Japanese in my boyhood days had the near monopoly of another market—very cheap small toys that really worked. We used to find these marvels in the penny candy counters, rolled with two rock-like candy kisses in a thick piece of colored paper printed with the name of the conglomeration: "GUESS WHAT." All for one cent.

Though we stretched our boyish psychic powers to the storekeeper's snapping point, there was no way of guessing the prize within the mysterious "GUESS WHAT" wrapper, but it was usually pretty good, we all agreed. It might be a bird whistle, a cricket noisemaker, or a tiny clamshell that opened in a glass of water and floated an American flag underwater on a thread. Or it might be our favorite, a rubber and metal water pistol the size of a boy's thumb," which squirted water a good ten feet.

The most mysteriously interesting prize to me at the time, however, was a small white envelope labeled "Sun Pictures." Inside was a photographic negative—a crowd scene of some kind—and a piece of glossy white paper. Instructions were to hold the two together and face them into the sun for five minutes, to burn in the image.

If you did it right, you were rewarded with a real photograph print you had made yourself, and which, if kept away from the sun, might last indefinitely.

It takes longer than five minutes to burn permanent new goal images into our minds, and this fact discourages many who like their gratifications served up fast. So how, in fact, are we to go about imprinting goals in our minds?

Must we drown our minds in boredom first, memorizing obscure formulas, beating our brains into dazed submission, chanting mantras that sound like slightly drunk positive thinking? ("Every day, in every way, I am getting better and better."—Emil Coue.)

Do we just pour warmed over buckets of upbeat words on our heads when the moon is full, in hope of making some subliminal change in our "natural" behavior?

Or is there some simpler, surer, possibly interesting, even exciting way to go about this business, this business of changing our future fortunes by changing the mind's present picture gallery of its goals?

It happens that there is, and it traces back at least as far as the cave pictures painted by those prehistoric goal-setting hunters. How did they communicate those goals to their less visionary neighbors, whose cooperation was necessary to a successful hunt, but whose skill at visualizing abstractly was not too polished?

If the example of all cultures recorded since those early days is any guide, these goal-ideas were expressed around the communal fire in song, dance, and story. And what are singing and dancing but other ways to tell a story?

Story-telling is a powerful communicator of acceptable ideals (goal-images). Youngsters today go to summer camps partly because their parents want them imbued with certain cultural and religious ideals and know these can be taught or caught effectively around the ritual campfire. Back in our cultural infancy the fireside story was the only way we had to share goals across generations and groups of people.

Our hard-wired genetic programming for storytelling is so strong that the quiet phrase "Once upon a time..." can silence a roomful of rowdy youngsters and have them waiting expectantly for what may come next.

If you are on a long elevator ride and one person starts to tell another a story, notice how the carload of passengers lapses into listening silence. And if the storyteller gets off at an early floor, how disappointed the listeners seem.

Storytelling communicates visions, dreams, ideals, and goals from one person to another. The same skill can communicate it from one part of our being (our conscious mind) to another (our subconscious mind). This is how you can plant goals deep into your innermost self, without tedious memorization and hoping that you don't forget, to see them become part of you. And later part of your accomplishments.

Inner storytelling is another way of describing what Norman Vincent Peale calls positive imaging and what I have been calling goal-picturing. It does not require that you jeopardize your social standing and society's perception of your sanity by really talking to yourself. It does require that you create a dramatic story (scenario) for yourself, which helps you strongly and frequently visualize yourself in the process of realizing your most-deeply-felt BUT MEASURABLE goals.

This personal script, which you need not tell to another person until you achieve your successes, nor even then if you prefer, must become your substitute daydream, your salve when life bruises you, your inspiration when others laugh at you.

Let me tell you about my first personal goal-script, the one that changed my life radically in the space of seven months. It took me from an income of $14,700 to one of $89,400 the first year and four times more than that in most years since I first unreeled my goal-script in my mind on July 16, 1968. And it has helped me raise more than $2 billion for charity since I started.

At the time I was working for Arthur S. DeMoss, a genius in direct mail insurance marketing, the very father, in fact, of the industry, whose first successful effort had been the selling of hospital insurance by mail to nondrinkers. He was a man of deep Christian motivation and a philanthropist of the highest order. He gave me "free millionaire lessons," as I was later to call them, and much encouragement until his untimely death fourteen years later at fifty-three.

Arthur hired me to be his assistant for his religious and charitable projects, with a second job as president of a subsidiary advertising agency. He also gave me a book which was to have fateful consequences for my life. It was Napoleon Hills *Think and Grow Rich,* which I obediently read and laid aside.

Meanwhile, with Art DeMoss pushing me to grow, I crisscrossed the nation with him and others, conducting seminars for religious nonprofit groups on the raising of money by mail. Art always put his money where his heart was, so he gave seed funding to many groups to help them become more self-supporting, and I would help them get started in their new or expanded direct mail fund-raising programs. In the process I became one of only two or three persons in America able to work successfully in this national arena at the time.

In early 1968 Arthur decided to take his insurance company public, to get its stock registered and sold on the over-the-counter market. As a corporate executive I was to be assigned shares worth about one hundred dollars. When the appointed day came and went, though others got their stock, I did not get mine. This was not deliberate, only an error in computer entry, but it caused me to rethink my future. By the time my few shares arrived I was rereading Napoleon Hill.

In a two-day span I struggled over every word he wrote, trying to extract the essence of what Hill had claimed to discover. On July 16 I reached some conclusions in a high heat of insight.

I took out a yellow legal pad and a red felt-tip pen. As Hill instructed, I set forth the following:

- My goals for the rest of my life.
- A way of measuring achievement of those goals.
- A statement of what I would give of value in exchange for what I would get from life.

My goals also were three, and I shall get to them in a moment. Only one of them, as it turned out, was measurable, and the measure was money—a nice, round hundred thousand dollars. If it showed up, there would be no mistaking its presence. No guesswork was involved.

My give-and-get statement of equitable exchange with life, which Hill wisely insisted upon, came to be expressed as part of the goals themselves.

The first goal was utterly, wrongly subjective, demanding something there was no way to measure, hence really no way to achieve under any of the rules of Positive Thinker's Goal Setting. I set forth that I wanted TO BECOME THE BEST DIRECT MAIL FUND RAISER IN NORTH AMERICA (hence probably the world as well).

Admirable? No doubt. Vain? Not a little. For there exists no qualified authority to confer my crown if I won it. Through the years I have won my share of awards, true, but not in the nature of a World Series, where only one winner is possible. Had I declared to myself that I wanted to win a Nobel prize for fund raising, this would have been a true goal for our purposes, being objectively measurable— however astonishing—if it happened.

Had this been the only goal I wrote down that day, I would not be writing this book today. And I might still be working for someone else.

My second goal was equally lofty, but not much more measurable, as I realized years later. (It was the third goal that saved me.) Goal Two: TO HELP AMERICANS

MAKE BETTER USE OF THEIR LEISURE AND RECREATIONAL TIME.

I was aware people were starting to live longer and were working fewer years. All this represented a potential waste unless someone could devise ways to harness all this unutilized people power to good causes. I volunteered to be the good fellow who would make it all happen. But this was not a true Positive Thinker's goal, as we have seen, being essentially immeasurable

One happy byproduct of this misspoken goal, however, was my later creation of large international congresses and unique overseas travel events which thousands attend each year.

None of this would have happened, however, had it not been for my boldly stated Third Goal: ACQUIRE ONE HUNDRED THOUSAND DOLLARS IN WORKING CAPITAL IN TWO YEARS.

Now there was a goal that made me quake. It was not easily spouted like the first two. It was measurable both in dollars and in days. At the rate I was then going, it would take me twenty-five or thirty years to acquire such a sum to set myself up properly in business. This was a GOAL!

Yet I was to achieve it in less than six months and be successfully launched in my new business one month later, spending all of $2,000 to get started, not the $100,000 I had thought I would need and now had on hand.

Two years and eleven months after I wrote out my goals and first played out my goal-story to myself, I stood on a hill in Jerusalem, watching 2,000 Protestant pilgrims board busses to return to thirty-eight countries at the end of a religious congress I had conceived of, financed, and promoted. It had been one of the largest international Christian conclaves in the Holy City since Apostolic times. The founder of the

State of Israel, David Ben-Gurion, had been our keynote speaker, as the *New York Times* and *Newsweek* reported.

It had taken me $40,000 to bring off this Jerusalem Conference, which passed close to two million dollars through the books of my three-person corporation, of which $80,000 was profit. I kept $20,000 for the business and gave the rest to charities.

I report this so you can have some appreciation for the potential large consequences of personal goal statements, even one as riddled with flaws as mine was. Perhaps you would be interested in the scenario I scripted for myself that July day that energized my subconscious mind to make my goals become realities.

It was not some grand and noble script, I assure you. It did not read like poetry or like something you should engrave in marble for posterity's edification.

It concerned my perceived need for $100,000. First I took out a couple of dollar bills from my wallet and put them on the kitchen table. Then I imagined what 100,000 of them would look like. It was too much, too messy. I tried it with tens and finally with completely imaginary $100 bills—1,000 of them.

My purpose was to envision repeatedly and dramatically what $100,000 truly looked like. If I could encompass it in my conscious mind, Napoleon Hill said I would be able to make my subconscious mind accept the assignment of finding me some honest way to let me earn it.

For a day or two I struggled to make myself "see" $100,000 on the table or my desk. It was boring and about as much fun as taking a prescription every four hours. So I changed tactics with myself. I created a story line, a little movie if you will, a scenario, with me, my banker, and my money. (Well, it was going to become mine, I was sure of that, if I could just get in touch with my subconscious mind somehow and put it to work!)

Today, years later, this little event in my life, that never really happened, is more real—and has had more effect on my life—than thousands of things which verifiably have occurred.

In my fantasy script, this story I am telling to another part of my mind, I see myself as already being in possession of this useful pile of cash. I hear myself call up the banker in the little green town a few miles down the valley, saying "Ernie, this is Gaylord Briley. I'll be coining in later today to pick up my money and take it for a ride. Get it ready for me, will you?"

As real to me today as though the event truly happened (which it did not need to, once its purpose was served) I can see myself riding back to my house on the ridge, with the cash banded neatly and sitting in a cardboard box next to me. I take it into the kitchen from the garage and carefully stack it on the table. The sunlight of my imagination splashes through the trees outside the window upon my precious capital next to the toaster.

After a time I gather up my money, putting each packet of bills back in the box and drive my hard won resource back to the loving care of my friendly banker, who is nervously waiting to put it back in the vault.

Ridiculous you say? A grown man playing make believe with himself, conjuring up images of money he does not own ... and has no clear idea of how to get! True, all true. But it served me admirably as your own goal-script will serve you. Mine gave my underemployed subconscious a purposeful goal to achieve. I was enabled, by this story stratagem, to visualize my money need so strongly and so often that my working mind had permission and authority to find lawful ways to garner $100,000 and go on from there.

How I finally got the capital seemed almost anti-climactic when it came. A new national travel agency asked me to freelance write a letter that might persuade clergymen to lead Holy Land pilgrimages through them instead of their well-established competitors. I wrote one that got 27,000 affirmative replies out of 130,000 mailed. (This was the first—and so far as I know, the LAST—sweepstakes mailing ever aimed at the clergy.)

The company was spectacularly launched, and to induce me to keep working with them, they gave me shares in the firm worth more than my goals required.

This, like many of the wonderful things that have happened in my life since, I can trace to the day I found a way to make my newly-declared goals come to life for me.

I did it the way the cave artists at Lascaux did 150 centuries ago: I visualized the objects of my desire and made them real to my inner, goal-striving mind. That was how I changed my future. IE is how you can change yours.

Posi/Thoughts

What we visualize, we tend to do or become.

Failure images in the mind can only be displaced by good goal images, never just driven out.

By burning into our minds the goals we picture, we can work towards success 24 hours a day, since that part of our brain does not sleep.

Make goals run your life by embodying them in an inner movie or TV script repeatedly played back in the mind.

A Positive Thinker's
Goals Must
Always Be
• Measurable
• Life-Enhancing
• Specific as Possible

CHAPTER EIGHT

STEP FOUR
Positive Thinking:
Self-Programming for Success

Comparing the Positive Thinker's success-process with computer systems earlier, we saw we would equate "Positive Permission" with a personal computer's on/off switch, "Goal Setting" with keyboard entry, "Goal Imaging or Positive Picturing" with the computer video display or screen, and "Positive Thinking" itself as the computer program which makes the whole system function.

All computer programs have to be written in some kind of "computer language" (e.g., BASIC, FORTRAN, COBOL) in order to communicate to the Central Processing Unit the work that needs doing, the problems that need answers.. Various languages have been created to deal with different levels of computer capacity, different kinds of problems to be solved.

A language that helps to write programs that design automobile bumpers might not run the word-processing program of the computer on which these words are written. Computer languages tend to be fitted to their tasks and the equipment on which they must run programs.

The Language of Positive Thinking

A computer language is really a vocabulary of possibilities. The language describes, and sets limits to, what a programmer and a computer are able to achieve. No computer (or human mind) can deal in concepts for which it has no symbols. Results can only be given in terms of those symbols.

So there must be an underlying "computer language of the mind" that enables Positive Thinkers' self-programming to achieve its long-reported results. What is it?

It has to be a "language" whose symbols and connective logic make positive input and positive output easier than earlier languages. It has to have a vocabulary based on nouns such as "goals," "purpose," "attitude," "faith" and "achievement." Its verbs have to include "give," "believe," "share," "think" and "help."

It has to be a "language" that makes it easier for people to think positively and efficiently about their own life-enhancing goals... and then obtain them.

Most of us already know this language, or a good part of it. The language of Positive Thinking is the language of SUCCESS!

All cultures and social groupings develop vocabularies of words describing things important to them. What is more important to Positive Thinkers than success?

We give names to what is of concern to us. Primitive tribes do not always have words naming, for example, numbers above a certain point. They own so little that can be tallied, and are so few in number themselves, their counting may be limited to "One, Two, Three... and Plenty."

Anthropologists are aware of cultures that lack words for more than three or four colors. To these remote peoples, half the colors of the rainbow have no name, or are smudged together as a color group, there being no use for these extra words in that particular culture.

Then there are peoples who develop many words for a subject that other groups dismiss with but one or two. The maize-growing Mayans and other cultures dependent on corn crops for their basic diet might have twenty or thirty words for corn, each one describing the plant at a particular stage of its growth or state of preparation.

Likewise descendants of potato-raising Incas in South America have dozens of names for that humble tuber, because each name encodes a complete understanding of the condition of the crop. The reason they have so many words and we but two or three for the potato, has to do with its relatively greater importance to their survival than to ours.

The more words people have for a subject, the greater its importance to them. The Inuit peoples (Eskimos) of the Canadian Arctic have numerous words for snow. Each word is an encyclopedia of meaning, conveying the snow's crystal size, accumulated depth, age, water content, safety to walk or sled on, and the possible presence of seals and fish below the ice or polar bears above it.

The Positive Payoff

Positive Thinking is an inner computer language of the mind that deals with attitudes, goals, rewards, new ideas, accomplishments, mutual help, benefits and the future. It is programming that deals with these subjects AND PAYS OFF in them. (All programs pay off in terms of whatever they deal with.)

If one uses Leninism as a mental computer language or symbol-manipulating system (and some do) the payoffs will come in things that Marxist-Leninist symbols deal with: mass murder, appropriation of other people's legitimate earnings, contrived revolutions, social disorder, and rigid control of society once power is achieved... plus privileges for those who brought about this state of affairs, if they are not killed first.

Language determines goals and payoffs. The language and, therefore, ultimate aim of Positive Thinking is success.

This presents a problem to some people, among them many women, who understand success, wrongly, only as the result of push-and-shove competition. They avert their eyes from success as a goal, believing that it is rarely achieved except as the result of hurting someone else.

This bias runs through much of contemporary life and accounts for popular entertainments that depict successful people as scoundrels hiding behind unearned wealth. This bias explains the astonishingly open class hatred traded on by some politicians who seek public office by boldly promising a presumably jealous electorate to pass tax laws punishing those who achieve financial success. They think voters secretly believe anyone who is successful is a crook.

By any definition in any dictionary, this understanding of success is wrong. Success is *merely the favorable termination or outcome of effort.* That effort may be learning to play the piano, work a computer, or establish a new business. Success can be a good grade on a report card. Success can even be a good marriage.

Successful people are not necessarily wealthy. Nor are all wealthy people successful. Anyone CAN be a success, because God obviously organized us to achieve it. Everybody SHOULD be a success, because that causes us to grow and stretch our limits, without needing to hurt others in the process. (Unless you count those who are not pleased with YOUR growth because it spotlights their own failure to grow.)

In Europe, the person of inherited wealth is taught to disdain manual labor. The same is true in parts of Asia and Africa, among those who go through the forms of higher education. To demonstrate their superior status to those not able to read their credentials, they make great show of demeaning labor with the hands.

The equivalent attitude was formerly found in many North American schools, where financial success, rather than manual labor, was the object of fashionable sneering.

Many educated in the Drop-Out Generation a while back fled to communes and other places where they COULD work with their hands to repent of being the offspring of successful parents. To a whole generation, the idea of business or professional success was poisoned. In place of success, they sought self-sufficiency, finding guilt in the money that made their life possible, money they themselves did not understand how to make.

Those days are over. Instead of a guru, the fashionable now seek an MBA at Wharton or Harvard. It's acceptable now to become an entrepreneur, go into business, and become a whopping success. Especially for women.

Still, the malady lingers on. Many still have not heard that success is good for people, that the Surgeon General does not require health warning notices printed on our goals.

The Positive Thinking Heartland

America turned out to have the perfect soil to grow Positive Thinkers. Having no mistaken pride of ancestry—being a race of discontented immigrants the Old Country

85

was usually glad to be rid of—Americans have always shown less concern with *who they are* at any particular moment, and more concern for *who they are going to be* someday. If not themselves, then for their children at least.

The Great American Positive Myth concerns the low born individual who, alone and by dint of stubborn faith in himself, makes a great success in life, despite adversity.

Our British cultural ancestors had no such universal myths about poor boys rising to the top, just a single tale about one "Little Dick Whittington, Thrice Lord Mayor of London Town," who died in 1423. A shrewd "Poor Richard" long before Ben Franklin's literary creation, a poor lad who worked his way to wealth, Whittington died a rich merchant, generous philanthropist, and beloved politician with a most improbable start in life.

As a young orphan he ran away from a dismal existence in London, only to be drawn back from his runaway path a short way outside the city by the sound of church bells, in whose tolling he heard a clear voice prophesying his triple destiny as Lord Mayor. (He made it by forty, again at forty-eight and once more at age sixty-one. Since only a person of substance and reputation could be elected, he must have made his fortune early.)

In the voice of the bells Richard Whittington heard enough to give him "permission" to overleap his humble start in life. He returned to London and made good. He also made the pages of *McCuffey's Reader* where generations of upwardly aimed young Americans met him as a reading lesson in their classrooms four centuries later.

After cutting literary teeth on *McGuffey,* for whom Dick Whittington was just one positive exemplar among many, it was easy for young readers to digest the magazine tales and books of Horatio Alger and others who added steady reinforcement to the idea of positive goals leading to positive actions justly rewarded with positive payoffs.

If it were not for America, Positive Thinking might have been longer developing. It grew up a sheltered plant under the canopy of Judeo-Christian beliefs, which stress individual responsibility to God. What a person does, counts. And God does the counting... with a final tally to be rendered on the Last Day.

Contrast this self-responsible framework for life with that provided by religions of the East. Most Oriental faiths, whatever their spiritual consolations and material benefits for devotees, proclaim a pessimistic world view where nothing good is lastingly possible, where personal extinction is the highest goal (because otherwise one keeps getting recycled for another go at this planet), where eternal life, even as a gift from God, is considered pointless.

Christianity and Judaism encourage individual responsibility before God. This responsibility bestows a powerful purpose on life: pleasing God and helping our fellows to do the same, knowing we get only one go-round and a record is being kept. Positive Thinking contributes to purposeful living. It fosters life-enhancing goals and daring achievements. It extends our faith and power.

As such. Positive Thinking, to paraphrase Norman Vincent Peale again, is not for sissies. It is not an elegant ruse to disguise failure. It is not a way of enjoying in the mind what one will never see in solid substance. (That is another name for daydreaming.)

Positive Thinking is a process, not an end in itself. It is no substitute for real life. It makes real things happen, things that would not happen otherwise.

How Positive Thinking Works

As "programming" that makes positive goal-setting work, Positive Thinking is bound by certain laws. They are natural laws in the sense that man did not invent them, but discovered them. They seem to exist because we do. They are spiritual laws in the sense that they work on the universe around us in ways that cannot (as yet anyway) be quantified, measured, or weighed. Only their effects can be discerned.

We are somewhere, with Positive Thinking as software (or lifeware, if you will), where scientific knowledge about electricity was in the years following Samuel F. B. Morse and his telegraph, yet before Alexander Graham Bell with the telephone and Guglielmo Marconi with wireless radio. We know how to get practical work out of the system, but it is not perfected. Greater progress lies ahead as we discover how to deal with this way of extending our power to change the world about us and tomorrow as well.

For all we know—and here the scientifically inclined should pause for some reflection before launching an attack— Positive Thinking as a kind of mind-computer program MAY be something as simple as *the most efficient way to utilize the brain* as *a physical organ.*

We humans are fearfully and wonderfully made. Who is not to say, without a lot more study and experimentation, that Positive Thinking works so well because it exploits our hardware (our brain and nervous system) to the best advantage? That it gets the most out of what we've got?

If you consider Positive Thinking as a way to pre-test experience (without risk to life and limb because you harmlessly visualize in advance what you want to do, without endangerment) it could well be that Positive Thinkers have enhanced chances for survival as well as success. To take risks mentally, before taking them physically, reduces exposure to physical risk, and also is a kind of rehearsal for success.

The more we rehearse our experiences ahead of time by means of Positive Thinking, the greater our likelihood of success. Practice improves odds in almost everything.

Yet something more is at work here than what goes on inside our brain, nervous system, and each sparking neuron. Something is going on outside as well. Some kind of natural or supernatural law of life. Peale speaks of it often in his writings. It is the law that *"Like attracts like."*

He has always been bold to say that we draw to ourselves the things that we pray about, think about, even worry about, because 'like attracts like." What fills your mind (or the circuits where Positive Thinking should be operative) tends to fill your real world as well.

In other words, sow hatred and you get it back. Plant cheating and you harvest the same. Disbelieve in yourself and you are certain to be right; you shall fail. But fill your mind with positive ideas, thoughts, and visualizations, and your life will ultimately be filled with the realization of these positive things.

What has stopped many from wanting to believe this law of like attracting like, is that it is at variance with physical nature. In physics we know OPPOSITES attract, LIKES repel each other. This has been clear to science since the days when experimenters still thought electricity was a fluid. Like electrical charges repel each other as do like magnetic poles. Opposite charges and poles attract.

While folk wisdom dotes on the same idea, that opposites attract, (poetically presuming lovers should complement or complete each other) marriage counselors will tell you the happiest couples tend to be those where the partners are much alike. Just as people like seeing themselves in mirrors, they like seeing their likeness in another person. Which accounts somewhat for the popularity of children as well as like-minded spouses.

How can we accept "Like attracts like" as a natural law if it violates nature? The answer is, it does not do anything of the sort. The problem is in our understanding. Our definitions are not fine enough.

We find little difficulty accepting that the formal laws of physics expressed by Sir Isaac Newton in the seventeenth century did not predict the behavior of matter at the level of nuclear physics, a science that would not flower until three centuries later. Learning that the laws of Newtonian physics don't neatly apply at sub-atomic levels became a scientific turning point that made further progress possible.

Which does not mean that the law of gravity and laws of motion formulated by Newton no longer apply to daily life. Our experience says otherwise. These are still important laws useful to mankind, But they are no longer the only books in our physics law library.

The observed spiritual truth that "Like attracts like unto itself" has nothing to do with how magnetic fields or electron flows behave. But it has a lot to do with how we should behave, for we only master laws by obeying them.

Only by obeying the then imperfectly understood laws of aerodynamics could the Wright brothers master them, leave the earth's surface at Kitty Hawk, and fly ... in apparent disobedience to the better known law of gravity.

Only by obeying the "Like attracts like" principle can we apply its power to our lives. When we do—and see the results—it will often seem in apparent disobedience to some other law people understand better, which no longer applies!

The "Like attracts like" law easily explains the success of Dr. Peale's "AS-IF" principle. He says if you want to BE happy, ACT happy. Act "as if" the circumstances were so, and it magically (it seems) becomes SO.

If you want to be bold in your actions, act bold and you soon discover you are. The "AS-IF" action is a very strong form of visualization, involving the whole body and its chemistry, not merely the brain. What we visualize strongly we tend to become or have or do.

Jesus taught the very same thing. He said (Mark 11:24 TEV), "When you pray and ask for something, believe that you have received it, and you will be given whatever you ask for."

Is not Jesus saying, *act AS IF you already have received what you are praying for... and your prayers will be answered?*

This "AS-IF" aspect to prayer could be God's way of testing for the sincerity of the one praying. Jesus may also be telling us to exercise our latent inborn spiritual gift, the "AS-IF" power, our power to create positive goal-pictures. These mental images somehow work within us and upon the outer world to make things LIKE them come our way.

If all the reasons for this are not as clear as we would like at this point in history, the problem is not with the reality of Positive Thinking's results, but with us for having been born a little too soon to settle the question.

This is the state of the art in our time. It works. We're not fully able to explain in mathematical terms to nonbelievers why it works, any more than we can explain why a wonderful poem or a song works. But follow the hard won rules and good things happen.

There are two ways to deal with what we know so far. The one follows the Russian model of licensing automobile drivers, the other the American.

In the Soviet Union the would-be driver must show not only a satisfactory driving technique and knowledge of road law, but must be able—literally—to take a car's engine apart and rebuild it, in order to be licensed to drive. One must be a mechanic as well as a driver

In America, while each state varies in some particular, it is enough that one knows the law and how to drive, and can demonstrate this in a road test.

The American may not know exactly why his car runs, but does not find that essential to get where he's going. Neither do you need to be a mechanic of Positive Thinking—able to explain why everything works the way it does—to apply its soundly demonstrated principles in your life.

Drive on!

The Inner Enemy of Positive Thinking

Friction resists every moving object. Expect a certain amount of it from the outside world, even in so laudable an endeavor as your use of Positive Thinking.

Most of us know enough to expect opposition whenever anything new and different goes on in our lives. Someone, somewhere gets discomfited if we change from being our same old predictable selves. We lose weight, gain credentials, acquire new skills, and it requires those who know us to open up our file again, make new entries in the log, and file us under new categories. That's work and people don't like it, if it can be avoided.

This kind of opposition we can expect and override. It is the INNER opposition we encounter that surprises us!

The worst enemy of Positive Thinking as your computer program for self-improvement is MOOD. Your moods will be your enemy when nobody else wants to oppose you.

There will come times when you really don't feel very positive about anything. The future will look tiresome and hard. The past like it wasn't worth all the time you spent there. The present will seem like a bridge of sighs spanning a seepage of blahs.

At that point, don't jump, pause. Just wait. For mood is a chemical thing. As your bodily chemistry unfailingly changes in the next few hours, so will your mood.

When things start looking dismal, it's time for action that will change the mood-madness sooner. Why do some women—so goes the fiction—go shopping for new clothes when they feel bad? Of course, it helps them feel better, they say. And they are right. (I go to computer shops myself.) Buying was probably the most irrelevant thing they could do at the time, but purposeful in its way. And just enough of an excuse to get out and change environmental input, which in turn helped alter internal chemistry.

Home a few hours later, they fee! better. But a few hours later they would have felt better anyway, no matter what action they took. Mood is not so much mental as chemical. Chemistry changes steadily in our bodies and minds. Our sleeping chemistry is different from our waking, our hunger chemistry from our sated, our worry chemistry from our joyful.

Like the weather, if you don't like your mood (chemistry), hold off awhile and you'll get something you like better.

Eating alters chemistry and mood, which may account for eating binges among the lovelorn and unhappy. As a writer I know I cannot eat sweets and expect to get any work done in the following four hours. My creative mind hits neutral and I get sleepy. So I work in the garden, take a swim, read the mail, or do uncreative paperwork until my normal self returns.

If you find your positive self disappearing at times it has work to do, don't get discouraged. It will come back by itself in a couple of hours, eager to pick up where you left off, if you don't yell at it. The thing you want to avoid is self-defeating doubt and overconcern. You are not the first or last person this will happen to.

The self-programming of Positive Thinking needs an open mind and a certain minimum of self-belief, self-acceptance, and self-esteem in which to function. If you find you have the qualifications at ANY time, then Positive Thinking can ultimately work for you; you have the equipment to succeed. Transient mood shifts cannot alter this fact. So do not let moods disable you or discourage you in your positive work.

Learning to use Positive Thinking to change the way you think (and change what your thinking nets you) is like going out for a suntan. You can't do it if the sun's not shining, so put it off for a better time.

Don't trap yourself into false feelings of failure. Don't let your enthusiasm wane because you feel different today than the last time you opened this book. Don't associate come-and-go mood feelings with your positive life-goals or you may feel like you've failed when you haven't even started.

Moods are not the reality of your world. The reality is going to be WHATEVER YOU THINK IT IS. The next chapter explains that bold statement.

Posi /Thoughts

Positive Thinking is like a computer language for the mind ... a vocabulary of possibilities. It is already familiar to us as the language of Success.

Positive Thinking's heartland is America, where people are less concerned with who they are than who they will someday be.

Positive Thinking draws its power from natural laws that are different in the way Einstein is different from Newton.

The great enemy of Positive Thinking is inside you, not outside, and stems from changes in mood, which can be altered or outwaited.

*Opportunity
Is a Moving Target,
And the BIGGER The Opportunity,
The FASTER It Moves!*

CHAPTER NINE

<u>STEP FIVE</u>
Positive Achievement:
The Reality You Create

After a quiet dinner alone in the suburban Washington home of one of the great political thinkers and fund raisers of our time, the great man and I fell into a long discussion, one that kept us both awake longer than we intended that night.

His servants had the evening off. As we cleared the dishes and stacked them in the kitchen I happened to pose the question. *Were the real achievers he knew, himself included, successful in large because they were brighter than average people by 10, 20 percent? Or was there something else to account for their achievements?*

Here was a man familiar to millions from the covers of news magazines, television interviews, and books, a man whom some reporter or another might call every half hour of the day to elicit his reaction to a breaking news story, a man whose drive and wisdom had forged a veritable communications empire out of nothing during the last two decades. At first he was silent. I wondered if something else was on his mind and he had not heard me.

By now our dishes were in the sink and he had tossed a package of popcorn into the microwave—our dessert. He said nothing as he waited a few seconds longer for the popcorn to stop making noise. As he poured it into a bowl and started toward the room where we planned to watch the network news on a giant project ion-TV, he had his answer ready.

"I've never been sure," he said," I am 10 or 20 percent brighter than average... or if I just work 10 or 20 percent *longer* than the other person. I can't say about other people. My only advantage may be that I'm up early working before others have started and work later at night. It may only be a matter of my personal discipline."

Self-discipline is the overlooked essential in most popular schemes for personal and social improvement today. The common failing of most so-called easy-loss diets, get-rich promotions, and self-improvement programs is that they do not demand the inconvenience of repeating a learning experience again and again, until it is second nature; nor do they demand more than token self-denial (skipping calories, not spending investment funds, etc.) as the price of success.

Earlier generations understood self-denial to be the prime act of committal by which one obtained a goal. Life then was so much harder, poorer, and briefer. Any goal demanding a commitment out of the ordinary called for a shuffling of limited resources to deal with it. Of itself, this rejuggling WAS self- denial. Knowing they had limits on their time and limits on their resources, people denied themselves some choices in order to make others they wanted more.

This truth is not so commonly believed in our time. Advertising and family attitudes reflected by the young say instead that "You can have it all!" (A belief in denying yourself denial.)

No one can "have it all," of course. One body can only be in one place at one lime, sleeping in one bed, eating one meal, or driving one car. "Wanting" may have no end to it, but "consuming" has obvious physical limits.

This widespread bedazzlement by the ample choices of life in America keeps millions (probably the 95-percenters again) unaware of their true limits until very late in life, to no one's advantage except those who find it easy to sell to the lifelong disoriented.

By denying themselves nothing, they deny themselves a chance for anything.

In the sense that all choices are open to us, we CAN have it all. But making one choice excludes others. A song from another day lamented this truth in a lilting refrain, "You can't marry ten pretty girls." One chooses. That means nine other choices dropped. And after choosing comes commitment.

All worthwhile goals require commitment and hard work to reach. This is where self-denial plays its role, by freeing up energy from less important activities to let you get your chosen, most vital work done.

What is "Positive Achievement?"

So far in this book we have held off dealing with a most important definition, a concept at the very base of our thought, and of Norman Vincent Peale's as well.

Not just "What is Positive Thinking?" or "What is Positive Achievement?" Rather, WHAT does "positive" itself mean?

My computer-side unabridged *Random House Dictionary* gives no less than thirty-one meanings to the word. And not one of them sounds convincingly like what we're talking about, even halfway down the list. Definition 12 is "emphasis on what is laudable, hopeful or to the good."

In other words, upbeat thinking is Positive Thinking.

Is that all? Are we just talking about hopeful thinking? Laudable achievement? There must be more. Otherwise we are deep in a trap Peale says to avoid. Positive Thinking is "not Pollyanna-ish" he has said countless times. It is more than doggedly discerning the darkless side of life.

Yet most of the other definitions are not satisfactory either. Definition 22, the mathematical, says "positive" is a quantity greater than zero. Not much help there.

Definition 30 deals with photographic negatives and prints. That needs further development.

Number 17, the electrical definition, we have dealt with earlier, in the fact that Positive Thinking as a mind-programming language is different from electricity or magnetism, for in its realm, like things attract, not repel each other.

Surprisingly, the biological meaning, number 23, could be one of the most useful: "Oriented or moving toward the focus of excitation." It at least implies action, movement, and growth toward a stimulus of some kind.

"Not speculative or theoretical. Practical." That is how definition 11 sees the word. Peale's Foundation for Christian Living has always presented itself as teaching "Christianity as a practical way of life." So the word practical fits, though it does not exhaust the meaning.

The synonyms offered are not much help: *Positive* = *clear, precise, definite, indisputable, unquestioning.*

If the dictionary were all we had to go on, definition 5 might have to do: "Confident in opinion; fully assured." It hits closest to pay dirt and follows the stream of Peale's public thought, for, as you remember, the successful book immediately preceding *The Power of Positive Thinking* was *A Guide to Confident Living.* The progression from confident to positive was logical and right so far as his public understood his message.

The philosophical entry, number 10, also has limited merit: "Constructive... rather than skeptical," as Positive Thinkers are always concerned for what is upbuilding and constructive. They are, as Robert Schuller says, "POSSIBILITY thinkers," far from skeptical about new ways of putting the world together.

Entry 15 considers positive as "proceeding in a direction assumed as beneficial, progressive or auspicious."

All these definitions are strangely without life! The impact of the term "Positive Thinking" has subtly changed the meaning and expectations associated with the mere words in the phrase over the last four decades. In time to come I think a new definition. No. 32, must emerge: Positive—as in Positive Thinking....

The enriched subtleties of the term, by that date, I leave to the lexicographers of tomorrow. But I might throw out to them a helpful hint, one that is fruitful for me. If they will hook up "Positive Thinking" with the meaning of the word posit (root of the words deposit, position, and positive) they might be on to something.

For that root-stub of a word describes more of what Positive Thinking does than any other in the dictionary.

Posit means to assume something as a fact or a principle. This is the very core of Dr. Peale's discovery!

Positive Thinkers ASSUME the reality of their achievement— long before it really exists—in order to MAKE it happen! It parallels Saint Paul's affirmation that "Faith is the substance of things HOPED FOR, the evidence of THINGS NOT SEEN."

A second meaning for posit explains something about why Positive Thinking leads to Positive Achievement. It means *to place, put, or set something down.* Again an apt description of what happens when Positive Thinkers go to work. Let me illustrate.

The Saco River starts in the White Mountains of New Hampshire and in passing through the Mount Washington Valley skirts the southeast edge of our pasture. "Skirts" is the wrong word; rearranges, transforms, or disrupts might be a better one. The river, at one vulnerable bend of land, is forever shifting its location, and my boundaries, for what seem the most trivial of reasons: a dead tree will fall or wash down in the spring flood and lodge on the far bank.

Because of that heavy mass positing itself off one bank, it redirects the river flow, causing the opposite bank, my field, to erode away. The erosion sluices ancient sandbeds and exposes hidden glacial boulders. The rocks cause the current to swirl, undercutting our alfalfa and timothy sod in readiness for a seaward adventure the next time the river rises.

It is the energy of the river itself that propels the sand, rock—and my property—along toward the Atlantic. It only takes one relatively minor tree trunk, posited in the right spot, to rechannel that energy and change the environment powerfully.

This is the very thing that the Positive Thinker is forever doing. By taking a stand, affirming belief in a new possibility, assuming something as a fact even before it is, he or she deflects others' energies around this new reality, making space for it to happen. Positive Thinkers get positive results because they don't have to do all the work themselves. By taking their stand, dropping strategic logs and rocks into the river of life, they harness its energy to achieve their high purposes. They don't get swept along like others because they have something solid to hang on to—their goals.

If we wanted to be technical, perhaps it would be wiser to call our concept POSIT-ive Thinking.

Can Positive Thinking Be Misused?

If we understand Positive Thinking as a mind-computer program that helps achieve our goals, we have to ask if it can be perverted to evil ends. Can it be misused? Is it possible to use Positive Thinking to injure others, deny them their rights, or limit their access to the resources of this present world?

The question merits asking because, as we have seen, some people are concerned that the successful exercise of their positive privileges may somehow hurt other people. So they withdraw from the challenge without trying, ending up the poorer for it, without having enriched the others or themselves by their negative choice.

That is the passive side of the question. The active aspect is, could some crazed 'Positive Thinker' become a master criminal by applying the techniques described in this book? The answer would have to be no. The effort would make him even

Symbol systems like Positive Thinking only pay off in terms of what the symbols are all about, because symbols tend to "tangibilize" in the person using them. Persons committed to promoting theft, fraud, and murder have to use symbol systems (Leninist, Mafiosi) that encompass such ideals. And they are very likely to be devoured by them. Misused tools tend to injure those who abuse them.

Goal-setting and goal-imaging are not limited to Positive Thinkers. Historically we ordinary people are rather late in using them. Once they were the exclusive province of those born to power or riches, not all of them nice folks.

With the wholesale democratization of privilege that has developed in our society where—for once in history—we can supply enough of everything for everybody, not just the privileged few, it has become possible for the rest of us to set and reach goals. Until our turn came, goal-setting was often exercised by some very wicked people (our "betters," of course) who conceived of some very wicked things... and inflicted them on the rest of us. That was their goal.

Don't blame this on Positive Thinkers. We *inherit tomorrow, not yesterday.* With nothing from the past to selfishly protect, we need not deal in symbols, goals, or images that will intentionally damage anyone or steal what is theirs. Becoming whatever we fill our minds with, as the Bible says, we who seek Positive Thinkers' goals can only be made better, not worse, for the experience. Positive Thinking changes people, but only for the good.

Are Positive Achievers Too Materialistic?

If you are a chicken in a barnyard, life gets dangerous the moment you distinguish yourself from the rest of the flock. They will peck you to a bloody death just for looking different; a red dirt speck on a feather perhaps. No room is left for apology, explanation, or repentance. You look different, you die. Your one-time scratch mates will interrupt their foraging long enough to beak you good and proper for your sin.

You lose your safety for losing your flock identity. The same thing may happen the moment you cross over the line and become a Positive Achiever. Your friends may not remember who you really are. You become something they cannot deal with. Positive Achievers are too god-like for them, making something out of the nothingness these people once shared with you. (That is their opinion, not yours. You will be hurt and surprised by their coolness.)

One of the ways they will express their displeasure is to accuse you, among your erstwhile companions, of the sin of "materialism." Some of them will make much of the Biblical statement, which they misquote, saying MONEY is the root of all evil. That is not what was said, of course. Rather, "The LOVE OF MONEY is the root of all evil."

It is also true that knives are sharp, but we find knives necessary and safely use them all the time. We're just careful and keep them out of the reach of children.

A poor man may do more desperate things for love of the money he does not own and does not understand how to make, than a regiment of rich. Muggers are rarely wealthy playboys on a slum holiday. The richest neighborhoods are usually the safest to walk in alone. Nobody there is ready to trade your life for the contents of your pockets.

So why are the poor considered virtuous and the once poor who are now a little less so, considered wicked?

Perhaps nothing more sinister is at work than the fact that most people do not understand success, they see so little of it first hand. And it is easy to dislike what you do not know.

This is another consequence of the 5 percent rule; 95 percent of the crowd has no idea success can mean anything except money to spend greedily on oneself. Whereas it is evident that Positive Thinkers know that money is only an activator, catalyst, enzyme, or actualizer that helps you get other things done for the ultimate benefit of others.

Money—the reaching for it, the spending of it—brings out the real person. It can be invested to enrich the lives of millions for generations; it can be wasted in rapid debauchery, paving the road to Hell with Teflon bricks.

The TRUE materialist, when all is said and done, is more likely to be someone poor and mean spirited who thinks material things would answer all his need. He, more than the better off, better hearted fellow who tried the poor man's attitude and found it does not work, is likelier to "trust in riches" than in the Lord. And that phrase is the Bible's description of the true materialist.

The Price of Achievement

Every success has its price. Every accomplishment its cost. Not the least of which is that, by doing the one thing, you did not do some other. That's the hidden cost, the one economists tag on when you spend your money on a toy instead of investing it in something that earns you money. The lost interest is your extra cost.

The Positive Achiever must have his goals, but it is always worth asking if the hidden cost of their achievement has been weighed into all calculations. When the children are young, you may not wish to embark on a time-eating project that could rob you of the joy of seeing them grow. Above all people, the Positive Achiever knows that life is more than money.

The hidden cost of writing this book is several million dollars. Not money denied to me personally, but to would-be clients, charities needing "break-through" ideas, whose direct mail fund-raising projects I had to postpone writing until this manuscript was completed. I weighed all the hidden costs I could see, made adjustments to my schedule, and went ahead.

The achievements we choose have their price. What most people do not know is that you can pay a lower price or a higher price to reach the same goals!

It is a rule of life that few regard, but *"The first price life offers is always the cheapest."* The longer you wait to pay, the more it costs. Sometimes the cost gets to be too much. It's NOT like a finance charge, where people may not mind paying its added, seemingly small cost for the convenience of lower payments over a longer stretch of time, even if the total price is raised by half. Rather, the base price you pay is itself increased, the longer you wait.

The personal cost of going to college is one price at eighteen and quite another if one matriculates at thirty-five in the midst of life with a family to support and a job to maintain. For many the cost gets to be too high after a certain age.

This lowest cost rule underlies the value of surprise in warfare. If an army can win its objective at first strike, its price in casualties and war materiel is usually less than if the initial strike fails. For then it can be expected the enemy will reinforce his position and shift his strategies to exact a higher cost the next time.

Sometimes the price of delay multiplies the cost so much and so unendingly as to make it necessary to transfer the costs to others.

Example: The failure of the U.S. government to drive a Marxist-Leninist regime out of Cuba in the 1960s, led not only to the brink of nuclear war in the Cuban missile crisis, but continues to exact a price from you and me personally and from every person who rides a commercial plane anywhere in the world.

Because we appeared to be weak, and Cuba offered a safe, close-in haven for anyone with a grievance, gun, and guts to commandeer an airplane, the endless epidemic of hijackings began. The price of this failure to protect our national interest has risen every year. And the government is not the one paying the price. You and I pay it. It is borne by each traveler in the form of added inconvenience, erosion of personal rights, added ticket expense for inspections and guards, and the terrorizing or death of some of us.

Our government failed but once to do its proper job and the rest of us, like it or not, are now stuck with a mounting bill, and the last payment is nowhere in sight.

Some may argue back that hijackings were inevitable and had it not been Cuba they would have started somewhere eke. Perhaps. But convincing action against Cuba earlier would have raised the price hijackers might expect to pay, possibly deterring them past our own lifetimes. Meanwhile, expect the cost to keep growing because we did not pay the lower price tag when we could.

If this seems a rather strong example to illustrate the rule that "The first price life offers is always the cheapest," it is probably not one any of us can forget.

Positive Thinkers do not hold a falsely benign view of the real world. If an example like Cuba helps us remember the first price rule and "redeem the time because the days are evil," as the Bible says, then at least some good will have come from this conspicuous failure to pay the right price at the right time.

Posi /Thoughts

The little-understood key to Positive Thinkers' success is that they POSIT their faith—affirm belief in new possibilities that deflect new energies their way and help them achieve their goals.

Success has its price, and the lowest price is always offered earliest.

POSITIVE LIFESTYLES

CHAPTER TEN

Life Is a PLUS!

If you believe life has meaning, you are, whether you know it or not, a religious person. I would hope this is not news to you, but for some readers it will be. They may never have thought of it before.

Most of us—I in the writing and many in the reading—approach the subject of Positive Thinkers' achievements from a tacit Christian base of understanding, for we believe that our life is a gift for which an accounting eventually must be made.

It has always seemed to me that surprise birthday parties were the most appropriate kind. All of us are surprise guests on this planet, landing hungry, with no baggage, met by a couple of bemused strangers who are a lot bigger than we are and don't speak our language.

We had no voice in our getting here, or a few of us might have spoken up for a quieter century. We have little to say about our time and method of departure. After we get used to the place, we are usually reluctant to leave, but we do eventually anyway.

Life is a PLUS! It's a totally unexpected boon. A chance we did not earn. An opportunity too good to pass by. How on earth can anyone ever get bored with it?

Not only is it fun and filled with other interesting creatures like ourselves (not angels, obviously, which makes them even more interesting), but the One who started the whole thing rolling sent His Son here one time, just to straighten the place out and let us know how important a place He thought it was, this world He made for us, (Aside to theologians: No disrespect intended, fellas, but I thought the handful of readers who were surprised they were really religious, and didn't know it, should have a quickie synopsis, to know where they came in.)

Our lives are bracketed between two eternities, one at each end. Yet God attaches an importance to what we do here in this physical realm in the brief hours of our earthly existence. Why? It must be something that cannot be done in another world, a world without physical bodies.

Christians believe they will continue their existence with God in the next world and that that is justification enough for this physical world to exist: as anteroom, testing chamber, sorting bin, or what have you.

I think there is a hidden truth here somewhere, a lump in the mattress of our complacent acceptance of this fantastic world we live in. The longer I live, the more I see, and especially the more I see of what Positive Thinkers achieve in their lives, the more I am of a feeling that our physical lives are holier than even the most stringently devout have ever taught.

In these tangible frames worth a few dollars in basic industrial chemicals, we live corporeal lives. We touch things, they move. We move matter from one place to another, either with sweat or by inventing machines to do it for us. *(Transportation is the basic activity of the universe, we are told.)*

A pattern is slightly discernible; the purpose is not, God holds it too close. All the commandments and exhortations aside (not to be ignored, they are there for our good), one is left with the sense that somehow what we do in this physical realm is very, very important to some eventual outcome. Only in this realm can thought be transmuted into action that moves and changes substance. Life is a condition in which the soul can perform miracles it cannot do when chorusing with angels on the door stoop of heaven.

Life is a PLUS... and it's being played for keeps.

*Life Lets
You Choose:
Goals...
or Controls!*

CHAPTER ELEVEN

The Positive Dilemma of
Today's Woman:
Color Me Dutiful... or Beautiful?

The conspicuously forgotten person in most talk about Positive Thinkers is today's woman. Yet she has invested more heavily in positive outcomes than men ever have. Now she is being derided for it and this fills her with confusion and uncertainty.

If we hitched a ride on a time machine back to those forgotten ages whose only record is in our genes, back before the first book was scratched on clay or the first city heaped together from the same material, and monitored the two sexes for their respective goals and Positive Achievements across the millennia, what would we find? We would find history's Positive Thinkers' Award going to the women without question.

Despite the wars, follies, and misadventures of men, women's biological programming (or good sense) has always nurtured the positive goal of ensuring the presence and survival of the next generation of our kind. This is a Positive Achievement of the highest sort, if one does not listen to the professional doubters who make themselves rich selling doubt *(negative thinking)* to the rest of us.

The early and continued success of a book like *Color Me Beautiful* (over three million sold) is one positive signal that today's woman is struggling hard to work out of the dilemma she's been locked into. For until recently, with rare exception, the only right color for a female was *protective* coloration: dutiful. That duty was to be so bound up with the man as to cast only one shadow. Or so she was told.

Today's woman is concerned about personal beauty and attractiveness as aids to survival. Having lost her supposed guarantee of a lifelong protector, she is forced to compete with other women, and men as well, for an income in the marketplace. In this arena her appearance counts in ways that can be measured in dollars.

Once the privilege of personal beauty care was limited to a wealthy leisure class. Now it, like everything else, has been democratized and made available to every interested person. But now the interest is not in beauty for beauty's sake, but in looking right when on the job and looking great when competing for a mate.

Today's woman almost certainly has to work outside the home for a major part of her life, no matter how old fashioned she may be at heart. To retain her femininity while holding down her new job and hanging on to most of the traditional ones at home, she needs all the help she can get. Authors of women's self-help books provide a new kind of practical guidance today's woman would never get from her own mother or aunts or in-laws. They are too rooted in the fast fading world that used to be.

The Wealth of Women

Nothing less than a revolution is going on. Society is thinking about women in a profoundly different way. This 180-degree turnabout is a turn for the worse for many women raised with the old ideals. Its very speed—a mere lifetime—adds poignancy to our cultural confusion about today's woman.

For most races and cultures through most of history, women were the true producers of the only wealth that counted. I am not speaking of places where women bore the heavier load in finding, raising, or preparing food. Nor referring to the wealth women generated by never letting their fingers be idle, spinning, weaving, and sewing.

Until very recent times on much of the globe (and in some remote spots even yet) wealth was measured not in coinage but in kin. Relatives provided that which money could not then buy—protection from enemies, food in times of hunger, care when one was old or ill. And the one source of relatives was, always and only, yesterday's woman.

Unlike today's woman, she did not have to fight others for a job to prove her worth. She *embodied* worth. She assured wealth through her ability to produce children, the one currency that could provide for everyone's need. Today's woman in that sense has been devalued. That for which 500 generations extolled her, is now often scorned. (The perception of children as expense, not wealth, shows in society's new attitudes toward abortion.)

She has to choose between work and children—as though children were a form of nonwork! Should she have more than one or two, she risks ridicule by the less fruitful when caught in public with her full brood. America is different from over-populated China only to the degree in which society punishes fecundity. There, those who dare to have more than two babies may lose jobs, income, and privileges. China is still too poor and too close to the time when children were a poor man's wealth, not a costly social burden, to allow the stork free enterprise.

In capitalist America, social disapproval of old-time motherhood gets expressed by lifted eyebrow, pointed finger, and snide asides at the shopping center.

A century ago everyone would have praised the mother of a large family with the Scripture, *"Her children rise up and call her blessed."* But no more. She is treated less like the "vessel of life," than the carrier of a disease called babies.

The popular theology of yesteryear taught that by bearing children, woman redeemed herself from Eve's sin. Today's woman is taught the opposite. All nonexploitive sex is okay, she is told. The only sin in sex is to have an unwanted baby: She might lose out on a promotion.

This is a sensitive subject, sure to be misread by a few whose inner anger over this quick switch of longstanding social ground rules may express itself in attacks on those who point it out.

My only reason for dealing with it in a book called *The Secret of Positive Thinkers' Success,* is to show the source of basic conflict affecting the Positive Attitudes of today's woman on the job and in the home. If a woman is forced to leave the home and work outside, she deserves to know why she is there. And if she needs to make a go of it on the worlds tough new terms, this book may help her.

In the name of her supposed ultimate happiness, she finds her choices for happiness officially broad, but socially narrowed. She may do anything a man can do, even compete with him for jobs. The one thing man CANNOT do—bear children, i.e., create a living tomorrow in which to invest new wealth and unfulfilled hopes—she is, as it were, socially taxed for doing. *(If you want less of any behavior, you put a tax on it.)*

Woman has been devalued. As a source of wealth she has been displaced by the machine and the corporation. If you want wealth, you go to where wealth is generated. It is no longer woman. "You want wealth?" today's man and woman are being told, "Go stand in line somewhere and take a job."

Some few will take a look at the length of the line and go start their own business instead.

A Handicapped Start

With access to wealth (abundance) no longer based on her body but on her body of knowledge, skills, and abilities, today's woman enters the job market from a negative starting position. She's behind before she starts. If anybody needed the Positive Thinkers' advantage, it is today's woman. If only to equalize her start.

Some women, if particularly blessed, and in the 5 percent potential superachiever category, will turn their unfair start into a boon. Starting from behind the normal toemark, they get a longer run in which to develop the momentum that can thrust some of them into great riches.

America is a strange new world, quite unlike the limited one our grandparents abandoned. In America, *if you want to become rich, it helps to be born poor!*

That is not a mere facile phrase. It is a reality that can readily be confirmed from tax records, a year's reading of the front page of the *Wall Street Journal,* or an honest appraisal of the income sources of families occupying the best homes in your town. Almost without exception you will find theirs is first-generation money, not inherited. The ones spending it are most often the ones who made it.

Their children also get good at spending it, enough so as to make believable the adage, *"From blue collar to riches to blue collar in three generations."* In America wealth rarely persists more than a couple of lifetimes. It either gets taxed away, divided into less potent parcels, or its underlying source erodes. (An industry declines, a natural resource is consumed, management fritters it away, lawyers consume it, a patent expires, or property drops in value.)

So, many of the wealthy try to convert their cash to forms that do not dissipate so readily. One of these forms is an expensive education for offspring. This would seem an enriching advantage to the following generation, but it has had an odd way of backfiring on the parents, due to the resentful anti-money philosophy of some who are paid to do the teaching.

One of Karl Marx's time bomb gifts to capitalism has been two generations of professors in high places who find only fault with America's economics and—sweet revenge!—inculcate their biases into children of the upper class.

With their unwittingly warped superior educations, these young people may learn how to administer (rule) but not how to make money. Their parents knew how. But the information got lost on its way to them.

By virtue of superior schooling, the scions of the self-made rich command high positions in our ruling society. But without the inner drive for success that drove their parents, they may unconsciously (even jealously) impede the rest of us by putting rocks in the road.

Today's working woman may find her road to Positive Achievement blocked by managers and administrators who offer her goals more fitted to their own well-fed class than to her real situation in life. She may be told to crave credentials for their own sake and not as tools to get where her goals or needs are directing her.

These educated offspring of the self-made rich, knowing little about the creation of wealth, want the rest of us to play life's power game with the marbles (symbols) they own—

credentials—white pieces of paper that do not purchase as much as green pieces of paper, like ostriches and penguins, they inherit wings but cannot fly.

If you ignore their attempts to redefine your personal standards of success, you are free to "wing it" to your own goals. Fear no unfair competition from those trained this way. If you are success-oriented, they are not headed in your direction. They can't often hurt you, but will rarely help you. Be grateful to stay out of their clutches. Being so misled about what is important in life (at least for you) they make poor guides to follow. The line to success does not form at their door.

In our wonderful world, the child of the poor (or the middle class) has a better shot at earning abundance—if that is her goal—than someone born to wallow in the educational lapses of luxury.

What Teacher Never Told You

Even if well-educated below college level, today's woman, as well as the man, will find huge holes in the fabric of their schooling. The system under which they were trained was intended not to produce thoughtful, goal-setting, self-productive individuals. It was designed to supply masses of model factory employees who are satisfactorily trainable for work machines cannot be made to do, and easily contented consumers who won't hurt themselves opening new product boxes. The ultimate finishing school for such a system is not the university but the army.

Which is not a sneer at a system which has brought more people than ever into literacy, handing them the key, if they will but take it, to all the learning of the past. For society and for most of us it has been a good thing... and some build on it to become truly educated persons.

But an academy of Positive Thinking it is not. And for today's devalued, disadvantaged woman who is trying to make something of herself, and make a place for whatever children she finds herself able to have, it is wise to understand this. Let her extract from the system the best she can, and start making progress toward her goals.

At its most effective, some say, the educational system was good at limiting girls' goals to those which, when reached, let them continue to be safely monitored by men. Examples abound. Nunneries, nursing schools, and typing pools share the trait of limiting woman's aspirations to specialized service ultimately controlled by men at the top.

The same might still be said of many jobs offered to even the most liberated female soul today. The giant corporation has opened doors of opportunity in middle management. Some women prosper there; others are burning out. Many of these new jobs once were the domain of the sidetracked male who had lost out in the greater struggle for corporate leadership and was waiting out his years to retirement in managerial oblivion.

These are vastly better jobs than women have averaged in the past, yet still not the best. The women who run them are probably more capable than the men they replace because they had to be, to gain recognition.

Precious few women ride the true fast track to upper management in the large corporations. Those who do find themselves steering through minefields planted by certain of the news media which pander to old attitudes by hinting that raw sex, not raw ability, buys their success.

All of which suggests that female Positive Achievers may continue to make their most remarkable breakthroughs in businesses they start or run for themselves. Here they can establish their own ground rules with no obligation to adopt the military ruthlessness often found in corporate life.

Parental Permission

We know that for men of high achievement it is often their mothers who grant them inner permission to excel and reach for their lofty goals.

New studies on women of high achievement suggest that for them, permission for unusual goal-setting was most often given by the father.

What encouragement to success can girls from broken, fatherless homes look for? We have not yet matured a generation of girls raised on a diet of "You can try for any job in the world." This slick propaganda now prospers in classrooms,

Scout troops, and comic pages. We do not know how effective it will prove, long-term, as a substitute for parent bestowed permission to succeed in life.

All children come into the world mildly afflicted with megalomania, believing they are invincible and all-powerful, or pretty close to it. Until they learn their limits, they are not safe to leave alone, as every working mother knows. Telling them they can do "anything in the world" may not be too believable to the youngster who has just spent 10 years painfully learning otherwise, and has the bruises to prove it.

Whether goals and morals imparted on the backs of cereal boxes or in noisy classrooms by uninspired teachers can substitute for loving parents in imparting permission for greatness at an early age, or only encourage more goalless, permissive behavior, is an experiment in whose outcome we all have a stake. Police records hint that we already have enough permissively raised children and undirected adults.

Without borrowing problems from the future, today's woman, because of traditions in effect while she was growing up, has a heavy stake in getting herself the permission she needs. Her girlhood schooling and family relationships probably are not much help. But the effective rules for permission-getting, which we discussed in Chapter 5, work as readily for men.

Special Problems and Goals

If Sigmund Freud himself was puzzled enough to cry out "What does woman want?" it is perilous for anyone to suggest goals for that half of humanity that previously enjoyed no great choice of goals to speak of.

First, regardless of gender, no person can take responsibility for another's goals. Influence them we do, as parents, spouses, friends, and teachers or coworkers. But responsible we dare not be, for the power is too dangerous for all concerned. When we start playing God we always end up killing people, however good our intentions.

Second, regarding gender, each girl or woman, in setting her goals, has to decide whether they will encompass any children she is biologically capable of engendering during one limited phase of her life.

Since society no longer counts her babies as wealth, preferring to generate its new wealth by control of sweat glands, not sex glands, the choice for or against children is more hers than ever before. As long, of course, as her goals include a way to raise them.

Her choices are also affected by the fact that women currently live seven years longer than men, on the average, virtually assuring most wives that some part of life will be spent alone, apart from the risk of divorce. Her goals—particularly those that relate to education, training, skills, and ability to earn—must deal with these risks of long life and loneliness.

This self-caring concern will be an alien thought to many women, predisposed (by nature or training, I'll not enter the argument) to do whatever they do FOR THE

BENEFIT OF OTHERS. It is well known that female embezzlers, for example, rarely steal to enrich themselves, but to aid some other person they see as needing help. They will steal to give selflessly, not to spend selfishly.

Self-denial by women may have had a certain survival value to the race in keeping children alive when resources ran scarce. A mother might choose to eat less so her young could eat more. But with society in its "Weight Watcher" phase, abundance splitting at the seams, self-caring is more important than self-denial for any goal-setting female.

"Goal-setting" means future-oriented. When every female produced maximal children, the future took care of itself. Or had to. There was too much to do today to worry about tomorrow. Self-denial squeezed out self-caring. Women who look to the future now must set their own clear goals. Failing to do this leaves them open to impositions NOT SO MUCH FROM MEN, as in the past, but from employers.

Like it or not, kids are still the key and the core to women's primary goal-setting decisions today. Her choice to have them is simple: Yes or No. If her answer is No, she is free to go on to her next goal.

But if her choice is Yes, three or four other choices have to be dealt with, for her goal-setting purposes.

1. Will she work for money OUTSIDE the home? If so, on what basis? Only before childbirth? Only after? Both? What about childcare while she works?

2. Will she work for money INSIDE the home? The option is new, made possible by the development of small computers, the home electronic office, intelligent telephone systems, rapid nationwide delivery services, and the like. Many new employment and business opportunities are

opening to bright and talented women who choose to keep one foot in the business world and one foot in the home while raising their children. More opportunities will be discovered by women with a positive bent of mind.

Even without the gadgetry that extends the business world into the home, many women are finding at-home income opportunities, providing services for a fee to their full-time out-of-home working sisters. These range from party and shopping services to the more traditional child care and making of products to be sold, from frozen quiches to knitwear run off on tabletop machines in the family room.

3.   Will she work only as a full-time, traditional wife and mother in the home? The choice to do this is laden often with strong religious and moral overtones but should not have to be held defensively by anyone, this choice long having been the accepted norm (or desire) of most Americans in the past. Today it takes money or sacrifice to exercise this option. With fewer men being paid so-called family wages, for many families there is no choice but for the mother to work.

Even so, a decision not to stay home is frequently made for fear of boredom, fear of loneliness, fear of missing out on what our society advertises as the highest good after *spending* money: *Making* money by holding down a job.

One who seeks the goal of traditional wifehood in the home today must also factor a new and disturbing possibility into her goal script.

4.   Will she be able to support herself (and children if necessary) if she becomes a cast-off wife? It used to be that the only worry a wife had, one

that an insurance policy could protect against, was the loss of husband and income due to his premature departure by death.

Nowadays he may depart prematurely for reasons no more serious than the dearth of his interest in the current household. For this there is no insurance, except to set backstop goals that seek education or resources for survival in case this happens.

These goals may fulfill a second need, like the storm cellar that doubles as food cellar. If she is left alone by his early death, the resource or education might lead to an interesting late career. (The Roman Catholic Church makes provision for late careers, allowing Catholic widowers and widows of good reputation, whose children are grown, to enter religious service as priests or nuns for what are called delayed vocations. One need not be a Catholic to find something admirable in the idea of a person at the far side of life embarking on a new career devoted to helping others.)

Applying the Five Positive Steps

Of the five steps discussed in our quest for the benefits of Positive Thinking lifestyles, all can be taken by anyone, male or female. They need some special commentary, however, since most of the writing and speaking on the subject until now has been male-oriented.

Positive Permission is perhaps the most difficult of the steps for many women. Kept under such restraints for so long, they may find permission to become different their largest obstacle. This being true, Positive Permission is probably even MORE important for a woman than for a man. It is the first step that must be taken, and like most first steps, the hardest. For some, it may be easier to begin by realizing that that for which permission is being sought is really nothing more than a RIGHT. We have a positive right to grow, to pursue goals and achieve them.

Positive Goal-Setting is still harder for some women because as a group they've had less practice at it. Also, many perfectly satisfactory goals were culturally off limits to girls and women for so long as to inhibit choosing them even today, when so much has changed. It may take another generation or two, with a few oscillations back and forth, before females and males select their goals from the same stack.

However, since the only real Positive Thinkers' goals (for our purposes) art those that can be measured in some way, there is a built-in bias toward male success, since their inner drives aim, psychologists tell us, more toward concrete things which can be enumerated, while women's drives run toward personal relationships that are harder to measure and number.

The challenge here for Positive Thinking women is to figure how to give their goals a measurable quality. For, when obtained, these measurable goals will have swept along with them in the slipstream, and delivered, all the less measurable good things that were part of the original desire-package underlying the goals.

Rather than saying "My *goal is to provide enough money for my daughter's college education,"* the goal should be made explicit in numbers. It is better to say "My *goal is to earn an extra $8,000 a year for the next five years, so, after taxes, lean put aside $6,000 a year for my daughter's career."*

(Note: If you raise a Positive Thinking child, she may have goals beyond being an obedient daughter. She may want to start a business with the $30,000 you give her, or invest it in the stock market, or take a trip around the world and deal with college later on her own, if at all.)

Positive Thinkers' goals must be expressed in terms of something you can number. If you cannot measure it, you cannot tell if you have got it all. Happiness is not a sufficient Positive Thinkers' goal, since it can only be pursued, not obtained. Happiness comes with honest achievement, and that is what Positive Thinkers work toward.

Don't worry that you seem to sound like a "materialist." The true Positive Thinker is never that. But this world is so constructed that the goals our spirits choose get expressed in measurable material things, whether we think we are comfortable with that fact or not.

Positive Goal-Picturing is a way for the Positive Thinker to rehearse reality before it happens. It is the way we get to choose which of the many possible onrushing realities we want to work with. We may not always get the one we want, but having a clear picture of what we seek, we can recognize our opportunities when they come and seize them. Any sex-bias built into the exercise of our imaging skills probably favors females. But it is a universal human ability, and as such amenable to improvement with use by anyone.

Positive Thinking, as the mind's computer language, has mostly found expression in male achievement terms (team sports, war stories, nature conquest, etc.) This happens because most nonchurch audiences for Positive Thinking were traditionally men's sales groups and men's booster clubs. This will continue to change, as Positive Thinkers' goals and word pictures and patterns reflect the experience of female self-sufficiency in the business world.

Until women left the home in such numbers for paying jobs, it was easy for cynics to scorn Positive Thinking—as they thought it applied to women—as a kind of plastic filler for low spots in the personality. To these critics, women were resorting to Positive Thinking only to deal with invisible, inward ills like self-doubt, depression, and bad habits. (An impression more strongly conveyed by the book covers and advertising than the book contents themselves.)

These applications of Positive Thinking not being measurable by outsiders, as we have noted, no one could prove the critics right or wrong. But women today are no longer the passive, inflicted upon, sorrowful creatures of past tradition (if they ever really were). So now it remains to be seen what they will make, and are boldly making, of Positive Thinking in today's larger, more competitive, more measurable—and more rewarding—world.

Positive Achievement. Until now, as we have seen, the greatest unsung practitioners of Positive Thinking have been women as mothers, who despite all negations and all losses, have, since earliest prehistory, provided us living bridges to a hoped for better future.

History itself, it has been said, can be told in the lives of only 100 people, most of them men, who evoked all the major Changes of the past 5000 years. No doubt some of the 100 were Positive Thinkers of a type; certainly all were goal-setters and achievers of one kind or another.

The unwritten record of woman's past achievement goes back as far as human traces can be found. The written record of her future achievement is being inscribed today by those who learn to apply the unfolding techniques of Positive Thinking to all other areas of life as well.

Posi /Thoughts

Positive women have been the human race's true source of wealth since long before history began. But the inversion of social attitudes toward women in one generation is placing untold strain on all women today and their families as well.

As a result of the new expectations imposed on women, they are more in need than men ever were of the power of Positive Thinking, and the personal goal achievement to which it can lead.

A Positive Woman's goals must include a decision about whether she will bear children. Or she risks letting others impose their goals on her.

The five steps of the Positive Power Pyramid readily adapt themselves to the needs of today's woman.

*If Energy
Is That Which
Creates Effects,
Then Money Is
A Powerful Form
Of Energy.*

CHAPTER TWELVE

The Entrepreneur As Positive Thinker:
Men Can Have Babies Too

I have dwelt, more than first intended, on the absolute necessity for the female would-be Positive Thinker to deal with her potential to have children. Not to deal with this central concern voids all her planning, all her goals; as we have seen, her life will forever be controlled by others. There is nothing quite like this fundamental choice that must be made in a man's life—unless he becomes an entrepreneur. The entrepreneur, whether man or woman, faces a commitment comparable to motherhood and love.

It will help to reflect on what love is: *Love is a commitment; love is not rational.*

No one sits down, draws up a pro-and-con chart to evaluate another's attributes, and on the basis of scoring personality traits (a seemingly logical, rational piece of behavior, considering the potential consequences) determines to love that particular person.

Love is, at heart, irrational. That is, we cannot rationally think our way into love, plan our way into love, even work our way into love, or fall out of it. Yet, let us hold in our hands for the first time a tiny, new baby that is born to us, and we commit to love it... when it has done nothing, as yet, to make itself worthy of our love. We love it anyway.

Love, the maternal variety or any other, is a commitment, "an IRRATIONAL commitment," based on feeling, not balanced judgment.

By the same token, entrepreneurship is a RATIONAL commitment. A commitment based on judgment and feelings expressed as a Positive Goal. A commitment to achieve. The way that faith is a commitment to believe. Faith and commitment are the twin components of entrepreneurship.

Heroes Still Live

The economic hero of our era is the entrepreneur. The word is French, the idea exquisitely American. One wishes there were another word conveying the same thought in less than twelve letters and four syllables. Economic heroes of an earlier time—like frontiersman-settler Daniel Boone and industrialist-inventor Thomas Edison—were idolized by those who hoped to imitate them. The hero our most un-heroic age praises is the entrepreneur.

Hero is the right word to use. The common image of a hero is of someone who risks himself for the good of another person or a good cause. The public sees him or her as someone otherwise ordinary and undistinguishable from the crowd who breaks ranks to take an unrequired but productive risk.

The entrepreneur really has nothing at risk but himself. He commands no resources but his own and those he has made his own by persuading his friends to help. He has,

134

in one sense, nothing to lose. Should he fail, he will find a way to get started again. (Only death or the death of hope can stop him.) But if he succeeds he is a hero. Professional corporate managers, who often succeed entrepreneurs at the helm, can never take risks of this magnitude, because they have at risk only their jobs, not their dreams. Having less to risk, they may reap less.

When commerce falters, the entrepreneur charges to the rescue with new ideas, new systems, new products, it is said. When his own drive and genius falter, if they do, he may sell out to a major corporation at a high price to retire in the sun or fund his next enterprise, because the big companies need his innovations to stay alive. Many giant corporations are really agglomerations of one-time entrepreneurial enterprises, the needlework still apparent under the cosmetology of the annual report.

Enterprise is the key, describing the positive boldness and energy of the entrepreneur in developing new products and new services for the new markets which grow out of nothingness in response to his innovations.

This is not quite the same as opening a small business, which the public seems to think it is, finding both equally praiseworthy. The elements of risk and marketing are as much present in opening a new hot dog stand as in designing, say, a pay phone computer for street corner use. But the creativity required, and the rewards possible, are of entirely different magnitudes. Profits from the stand may feed a family, those from the new computer might feed whole new industries, whole cities even, and those dependent on them.

The Positive Parallel

Both are alike, however, in the use they require of the underlying Positive Thinkers' technique of *POSITING*—

assuming something as a fact, before it really is, and acting on that assumption in advance. (See Chapter 9.)

The fact assumed is SUCCESS, of course; seeing the planned for result as inevitably coming to pass. This positing is more than mere hoping, for it has a basis in realistic planning and the underlying ingenuity of what is being offered for sale. Plus a lot of hard work. The moment of truth comes when the public encounters what is offered. Failure as well as success is possible, just as it is possible for love to be rejected.

By positing dreams, visions, and goals, acting as if these future things were presently tangible fact, the entrepreneur exercises the highest mode of Positive Thinkers' behavior... and is the cause of beneficial new realities entering the shared world of everyday life when he succeeds.

The entrepreneur is one who boldly risks all for a positive goal. What is actually being risked, however? Himself. Only that. And what he risks most is feeling troubling emotions about himself, like embarrassment, shame, and humiliation. These are chemical states of mind, if you will, emotions without permanent effect on the outside world except as he lets the transient flows of "fight or flight" hormones inside him deflect him from his outside goals.

Time is the critical factor. Solomon wrote in the Bible that "there is a time for everything under the sun." It is time, and time only, that determines how appropriate our actions are. The right action at the wrong time becomes a futile, sometimes even sadly comic act.

Robins do not nest and raise their young in December snowdrifts. The timing is off. Honey bees sense, to the hour, the time to visit different families of flowers to capture vital nectar flows at their flood. They do not waste time because, even for them, time is life.

One does not wait until ninety to start a family. You must live and achieve in life's allotted span. Our time is not a flat prairie of a place, but a rolling ocean with waves that come and go. You do certain things at certain times or never do those particular things. Not even the Positive Thinker/Achiever can bring back lost youth.

Time drives all of us, even a monster like Adolph Hitler, who found himself hitting fifty years of age in 1939. Knowing fifty to be "the youth of old age" he icily decreed the launching of World War II with the Nazi attack of Poland in September, overruling the concern of his military staff that they were not yet fully prepared for a long war.

Had war been postponed in 1939, circumstances might have worked against Hitler and kept war from breaking out. Millions of lives were lo be destroyed and millions more put at great risk because Hitler felt HE was running out of time. He told his generals he had to be young enough to enjoy his conquest of Europe and set up his Thousand Year Rule, so the war must begin while he had the vigor to pursue it. It was less important to him to have sufficient war materiel on hand or enough soldiers in training than for him to observe life's clock as it wound down.

Though he cut off millions from their rightful share of time, Hitler saw time's value on shorter horizons too, incorporating new concepts of timing into warfare through the *Blitzkrieg* the "lightning war" which used rapid modern weaponry and sudden attacks to shorten conquests to mere days. He sensed what many entrepreneurs instinctively know: *Opportunity* is *a moving target, and the bigger it is, the faster it moves.*

Time is neither our friend nor our enemy; it is something that gets measured out to us, to see what we will make of it. The Positive Thinker and the entrepreneur know that time makes all their gains possible, so tend to maximize the value of all the time they get.

This leads to a lot of misunderstandings, especially among the 95 percent who share the other 50 percent of life's optional bounty among themselves. They like to convince themselves there is something wrong, or at least mildly wicked, about the 5-percenters who create the other 50 percent and can be described as overachievers—thinkers who squeeze more achievements, results, income, and work from the same limited amount of time we all get each day.

The media, which usually peddle more papers to the 95 percent than the 5 percent, know which side of the muffin to marmalade. They spread failure folklore by larding it into feature stories that gratify the 95 percent mass. Thus we hear about capitalists and entrepreneurs being workaholics who court dismal death, sacrificing their family and home life by not knowing when to knock off work.

For some this is no doubt true. Particularly those who substitute working hard for working smart. "Hard work never hurt anyone," someone once told them. Right. But neither did smart work, and it's a lot more rewarding for everyone. Yet some feel guilty about success and cannot make themselves enjoy it without adding a sprig of suffering.

Successful entrepreneurs know something that most Americans have forgotten. They understand what leisure really is, and incorporate it into their work.

The true concept of leisure got lost somewhere about the time factories came into being. Before that, life was more closely tied to the rhythms of nature and the soil. So from the days of Greek glory to shortly after the day Thomas Jefferson died, a half-century after the signing of our Declaration of Independence, leisure was understood as being PART of work and life, not something apart from it.

Maybe nobody then ever heard of two weeks off with pay and retirement at 65, but they knew that if something interesting popped up during the day, they could in most cases stop their work to observe it or take part in it. They were not chained to production schedules and time clocks, so if the carnival came to town or there was a free public entertainment like a hanging up in the village, they had a good chance of taking it in. It was accepted that *work could be interrupted for the sake of OTHER enjoyment.*

A relic of this enviable past still clings to executive privilege, forming the most envied chunk of it. You sense how deep the envy runs by the way vote-hungry Congressmen think they can curry favor with the 95 percent by slapping punitive taxes on anything that remotely LOOKS like fun, pleasure, or play mixed into the serious tax-deductible business of working.

The work-play mix is apparently productive and good for business, however, despite the cynicism of the tax man. Deliberate leisure forms an important part of the seminars and planning sessions businesses put on for their executives at golf resorts, on cruise ships, and in exotic locales.

The business lunch is an example of the opposite, being an interruption of enjoyment for the sake of business. Entrepreneurs use business lunches to advance the cause, but many are just as happy packing a lunch and using the time to read the latest in their field or study the newest flips of tax law to see what barn door loopholes the emphatically anti-entrepreneurial tax wizards left open this time.

The successful entrepreneur is painfully aware of the 5 percent rule in life. He knows he is one of the 5 percent from whom 40 percent of the personal income taxes are extracted by the Federal government. He knows that in addition, at the business level, he pays an abundant share of the business income taxes, both of which the 95 percent have so generously voted to themselves. So he may be pardoned as a sensible realist if he spends more time than he would like figuring how to keep the business going and growing and feeding his employee's families despite the exactions of the tax man.

Put the entrepreneur's personal and business income taxes together and the stack shows that his personal efforts may generate the equivalent of half of all the personal income taxes collected!

Not bad for a disadvantaged minority—disadvantaged by the tax laws and a press that tries to paint the entrepreneur as working too hard for his own good. (If you think about his tax bill, he probably is!)

I know one computer entrepreneur, a certifiable genius in creating and marketing new people friendly computers, whose machines have lightened my professional load, who told me he would file the short form with IRS if he could, even though his income always gets taxed at the maximum rate. For he already has as his life goal the saving of the human race (in terms of computers and energy) so what if they take much of his money for taxes too? They are getting the best part of him voluntarily, so why should he care if they force a little more money out of him?

Not many people would be that altruistic, especially while working out of the second (seven-figure) bankruptcy in seven years caused by working with NONpositive-thinking, nonentrepreneurial associates.

The successful entrepreneur may be pardoned for not rigidly dividing work from play. The entrepreneur's work IS his play. He sneaks in his leisure by changing the focus of his work, by playing in the midst of his work. That, at least, no one has yet found a way to tax.

Money is Energy

After his use of time, the entrepreneur is best at making use of money, which is a way of transmitting energy across time to places where it is needed. *If energy is that which creates effects, then money is a powerful form of energy.*

If there were no other reason for the world of the entrepreneur and the Positive Thinker to merge as they have for many, money would be it. Money is so eminently measurable and useful, it lends itself to being a goal. It is a means as well, a way of getting things done. Money, properly used, is an activator of good things. It enhances life by concentrating energy that life may need in the future to save itself or others.

Perhaps there is no such thing as "too much money," only not enough goals.

Most entrepreneurs have clear goals and so have a good 'money attitude,' not thinking of it as Mark Twain said, as tainted. *("Taint yours and 'taint mine.")* It's theirs. They earned it. But to use, not just to spend.

The true entrepreneur is a practical Positive Thinker, dealing with risk and reward almost without stopping. Again the simile arises of the entrepreneur as a man who bears babies. His behavior toward his business is no different than a mother's toward her infant. She is totally aware of her child's wellbeing during all her waking hours, and has part of her brain "on duty" when she sleeps, to respond to its needs. Likewise the entrepreneur for his enterprise.

Whatever else they have going for them, entrepreneurs do not have exceptional records of marital stability. I mean, they appear to get divorced as often as other kinds of people in today's world. They do not seem any happier about this than other folks either.

Some of the marital weakness lies in spouses who actually resent the devotion their entrepreneurial mates lavish on the enterprise so dear to the heart. In marital postmortems you will hear them describe the business which tugged at their entrepreneur-spouse as though it were their sexual competitor. "If it had been another woman, I could have fought it," some disappointed wives will say, getting the picture all wrong.

Their jealous concern is misdirected, if it should be there at all, for it is infantile jealously that troubles them. The entrepreneur is not married to his work. The enterprise is not his lover; it is his child, and he is raising it. When it is raised, he will go do something else. Men can have babies too, you

Is It Soup Yet?

A television commercial for one of the dried soup companies used to show a hungry child peering at a steaming soup pot into which the dehydrated ingredients and water had been poured. After a time of hungry waiting, the child would ask the off-camera parent, "Is it soup yet?" Many ask the same question about Positive Thinking. WHEN does it cross over from being dry words and vaporous thought into actual, measurable, delivered goals? When does it stop being just a super idea and become soup?

I'm not sure an earlier generation, raised before the advent of movies, radio drama, and television, would have asked for such a clue, being better instructed about how the world works in real life. We've become so accustomed to the dramatic turning points, choices, and unseen perils of our story characters being asterisked by ominous chords and musical themes, it seems we can't recognize turning points in our own lives without offstage violins. The modern child at play actually sings out loud the theme music appropriate to his make believe activity, from "Lone Ranger" chases on horseback to "Twilight Zone" dah-dah DAH-dahs to indicate extraterrestrial contact. How on earth did kids play before movie music came along?

The person who has the most experience with the tangible results of Positive Thinking is, of course, the entrepreneur, whose whole life is voluntarily given over to making new realities out of mere ideas. Most of them I've asked tell me that it is like love, hard to describe, but you know it when it hits you.

Talking further, they usually add that they feel an up-tick in their normal level of excitement as they see the elements they planned—and a good many they never thought about, but expected to discover on the way—start to come together. So Hollywood is right in its way; they just use a musical "rush" to signify the physical one that is the first of an entrepreneur's many unexpected payoffs.

Excitement, by the way, characterizes conversations and life with the creative entrepreneur. Many of them are just exciting people to be around, especially if you get them going on their driving interests.

Perhaps the greatest entrepreneur I've been close to was Arthur DeMoss, my late (and last ever) boss, the one who gave me the free millionaire lessons at his direct marketing insurance company in Valley Forge, before I launched my own business. Art was an exciting, but unexcitable, man who was always willing to test new ideas. This willingness earned him a half-billion dollars.

Because direct marketing deals with large numbers of people, it is an unusually predictable business when done right. Art did it right. He would sample test markets and when satisfied with the results fearlessly roll out massive mailings and advertising campaigns to reap the harvest. His work motto was "RESEARCH, TEST, EXPLODE!"

His research (like most entrepreneurs' hunches) gave him a direction in which to go. Then he would test. He tested the insurance offers, the mailing lists available, the best day of the week to advertise insurance (for him, back then, it was Monday), the best color to use, besides black, in his newspaper ads (and that turned out to be blue, back then).

When Art was ready, he did what few others in his industry, or any other, have ever done. He literally exploded his campaign, making it the biggest, most powerful, most pervasive he could. He had faith in his research and in his repeated tests, which were always up-to-date and current.

Instead of putting the tests to anyone's vote, or asking the computer, as in most corporations, Arthur DeMoss, being the entrepreneur he was, had the faith to trust his knowledge and judgment. And he was right most of the time. Spectacularly

Underlying his excitement in his work was his faith in God and what God had him there to do. Just as the computer entrepreneur told me that his purpose on earth is to "save humanity" through the simplification of computers to help ordinary people solve the problems of living and provide more abundance for human needs, Art DeMoss would have told you his purpose in life was to bring people to Jesus Christ, who had changed his life completely.

The sketchy profiles of these two high-powered lives are not alone in showing that entrepreneurs are excited people, but more than that, they are often completely "sold out" to what they are doing. It is not a mere job. It is their high calling. What they are doing, they believe, is important and destined by something higher than themselves to help and bless others.

Don't Destroy the Feedback Loop!

There are achievers in this world who take a negative attitude toward the hurly-burly of commercial life. They wish to make their great achievements and bless humankind without getting commercial about it, preferring to get paid in honor not pelf. They desire to be great humanitarians like Saint Francis of Assisi, giving to others without getting for themselves.

Nice. And altruistic sounding on paper. But the world is not wired to work that way. If you stifle the feedback loop, disdaining to be paid what you are worth for what you do, you may destroy or postpone the very good you are attempting to do.

Case in point: Sir Alexander Fleming, discover of penicillin. We are familiar with his serendipitous discovery of the greatest wonder drug of the twentieth century, and how millions of lives have, been saved by it since World War II.

What most people are NOT familiar with is how Fleming's discovery lay UNUSED for years because of the seemingly selfless way he decided to market his discovery to the world. His mistaken altruism delayed penicillin's benefits for years.

Penicillin, you see, was actually discovered in 1929, but was little used anywhere in the world because all *the drug makers of England refused to produce it* until the demands of war led the British government to fund its mass production!

Why did no profit-ma king drug company produce this first major antibiotic when the world needed it so badly? Because Fleming, under the influence of the British system, which likes to think commerce is beneath the dignity of the upper classes, REFUSED TO PATENT HIS DISCOVERY, so everybody could reap its benefits!

As a result of Fleming's closing the feedback loop, denying profit to himself or anyone, nobody at all was to reap the lifesaving benefits of penicillin for many long years.

Because it was not patented, it could not be exclusively licensed to any one drug maker.

No pharmaceutical house would touch it on Fleming's do-good terms. In the real world, drug developers needed the protection of a patent monopoly to protect their hefty investment in a new medicine until it became profitable ... if it ever did. That last risk they would take, if only their investment could be protected meantime. At long last the government, under pressure of battle, made the investment that Fleming discouraged by his misplaced generosity, and his discovery started saving lives in large number by 1943.

For his great discovery, Fleming was later knighted by the Crown (i.e., rewarded by being made an honorary member of the upper class) but there are some who think he should have been given a royal boot at the same time for needlessly allowing other millions to die because he felt uncomfortable with the idea of profit.

It is better to be like my computer genius friend in California—let Uncle Sam pick anything he wants from your wallet, just so you are free to earn it in the first place—than to be like Sir Alexander and unintentionally pull the tubes from the profit-driven entrepreneurial heart-lung machine that keeps society going.

Positive Thinkers can pursue measurable goals other than money if they like. Most do. We don't all have to be entrepreneurs, no matter what the vogue. But if, in the process of reaching your goals, money is fed back to you by the system, don't try to stop it; don't wreck part of the feedback that makes the system work for everybody. You can always find someone to give the money to if it gives you problems.

To do otherwise is to risk destroying the very dream that underlies your goals. And why should any Positive Thinker do that?

Post /Thoughts

Entrepreneurs are the heroes of our time and most of them are Positive Thinkers by definition.

The entrepreneur loves his work as one would a child, as a projection of himself into the future.

The "feedback loop" which rewards success is best not disrupted, since it energizes the system and rewards everyone, not just the entrepreneur.

<u>STRESS</u>
Is Often
The Result
Of
Goal-Conflict
Or a
Lack Of Goals

CHAPTER THIRTEEN

Positive Partners:
[Success = PT²]

A new age dawned for the world the day an obscure Swiss government patent clerk named Albert Einstein inscribed his new theory, the most important scientific insight of our time, in a few, quick symbols: $E = me^2$.

It was a simple mathematical expression of a new-found reality: Mass and energy were only different forms of the same thing, he said.

Multiply the mass of anything by the speed of light, squared, and you had figured out the enormous energy contained in that mass, energy that could be unleashed under the right conditions.

A similar formula (Success = PT^2) describes what happens when you get two Positive Thinkers working in agreement to reach a shared goal. Their joint idea-energy and output are not simply added together; they get enormously multiplied. The two Positive Thinkers become equal in productivity to three, or four, or hundreds of ordinary people. Together they join the 5 percent that produce 50 percent of the wealth.

This mind-magnifying effect takes hold whenever two or more positive-minded people get together in agreement to seek ways to achieve a shared goal. It is not far from what Jesus said: *'Where two or three are gathered together in my name, there am I in the midst of them.'* What comes out of any Positive Partnership is much greater than what gets put in. One and one equal not two, but something larger. Problem-solving abilities are not merely summed, but squared, multiplied, amplified in some exponential way.

Napoleon Hill claimed the net effect was to get a supernatural bonus, an additional, superior mind helping you solve your problems. Which is amazingly close to what it seems like. Unfortunately, the more Hill says on the subject, the more he sounds like he's advocating a séance instead of a special kind of brainstorming.

He said to put together a "Master Mind" group of people united "in perfect harmony" to help you think your way to riches. Output from a properly run Master Mind group will exceed input, he said. You will find him right. Ideas come up that one has no right to expect. This extra energy bonus he attributed to outside spiritual forces which had personal names and individuality.

I cannot hold to his view about the source of the evident extra mental energy that comes out of a Master Mind group, and say it is dangerous for anyone to do so.

Rather, the extra mind bonus—the often unpredictable new ideas generated by a Positive Partnership—can be understood more reasonably as coming from the unaccustomed synergy of two or more eager minds, once freed from the haze of negativity that seems to surround most people.

You two, or your small group, as Positive Partners in search of solutions, should feel the rush of new ideas, not the flutter of angel wings, when you get together to Master Mind the problems in the way of your goals. Hill's lapse into spiritism is explained by his deliberate rejection of traditional religion due to unhappy contact with impoverished versions of it while growing up. Into the vacuum he inserted ideas borrowed from the occult East. This gave Hill a working scaffold to cover his real, yet rather inexplicable. Master Mind discovery, which is the Positive Partnership's great hidden advantage.

Ideally, a Positive Thinker will ally with like-minded people and a congenial spouse (if any) who will not sap with negativity the energy that should be zapping problems. It is hard to be the only Positive person in any crowd. So it is perfectly natural for Positive Thinkers to try making *Positive* partners out of the ones they've got.

More often than you might think, they succeed. When this happens, it is because of shared goals: Children to be raised, a living to be made, a debt to be paid, an invention to be developed and patented, a retirement to plan for.

Many Positive Partnerships go unnoticed and unsung. These are most often marriages, where it is decided, or understood, that one partner will be subordinate in the relationship for a time, to free the other to pursue a major shared goal. Thus a wife may work to put her husband through medical school, or a couple may cut expenses so the wife can finish her first novel without taking a new job. But Positive Partnerships are not limited to the happily married, by any means.

A Brother-Sister Team
In the case of Ruth Stafford, her first Positive Partner was her brother Bill. Their common goal was that each should have a good college education. This led Ruth to drop out of college for a full year and take a job, so she could help

Bill finish his schooling. The next year he took a job and helped her complete her degree.

So it happened that when she returned to Syracuse University, delayed a year in graduating, Ruth met the new, exciting—and unmarried—minister of the University Methodist Church, which she attended. Except for the year's holdup caused by her Positive Partnership with brother Bill Stafford, Ruth might never have crossed paths with this intriguing young clergyman. In time they were married and a powerful new Positive Partnership begun. The groom's name was Norman Vincent Peale.

If the truth were more widely known, Ruth Stafford Peale, as the positive life partner of Positive Thinking's discoverer, is no one's subordinate, being a strong leader and thinker and recognized international personage in her own right. It was her persistence, even to the point of rescuing his manuscript from a wastebasket when it was discarded by Norman in frustration and taking it to a publisher, that gave the world the book *The Power of Positive Thinking*.

Husband-wife teams, as Positive Partnerships, have long blessed the world in many ways. In the nineteenth century lived Heinrich Schliemann, a self-made millionaire obsessed with discovering the true site of the legendary city of Troy. He, the amateur archaeologist, wanted to find the lost site of Homer's Troy, dig it up, and prove to doubting experts that the city sung about by the blind poet actually did exist, thousands of years in the past, somewhere on the buried shoreline of modern Turkey.

A German, in middle-life he persuaded an Orthodox priest to find him a suitable young wife somewhere in Greece, to be his companion and helper in finding the lost Greek city. In seventeen-year-old Sophia, the girl he married at forty-seven, he found more than the answer he hoped for. He found a Positive Partner who fell in with his dreams, learned his language, managed his daily world, and dug with him for physical evidence of the Trojan Wars. And when he died, she continued his work. It was one of the great romances we know about... and solidly based on shared positive goals that motivated everything they did.

A Triple Partnership

Alive at the same time was one of America's first great engineers, John A. Roebling, designer of the then largest suspension span in the world, the Brooklyn Bridge, which opened in 1883. Its building is a tale of a three-person Positive Partnership, with one of them almost lost to history.

When John Roebling died prematurely of complications of an accident, the bridge which was to replace the East River ferry boats between Manhattan and Brooklyn lay far from finished. The construction—said by many to be too innovative and dangerous to attempt — was resumed by his engineer son, Washington A. Roebling.

He, too, was to face adversity. On an inspection of the bridge's underwater foundations, reached through primitive early pressurized caissons that kept the water out, the younger Roebling suffered the bends and was permanently disabled. As a wheelchair-bound cripple, he continued to direct operations from his apartment window a few blocks away, using field glasses.

At this point, history tends to overlook the third Positive Partner whose efforts were to make the Brooklyn Bridge, the Eighth Wonder of the World in its time, possible. It was Washington Roebling's wife.

Though untrained, she taught herself mechanical drawing and acquired engineering skills in order to be her handicapped husband's hands, feet, arms and legs in completing the technical marvel his father had designed. It was she who wrote the work orders, approved blueprints, communicated decisions to the workmen, and inspected construction in person the way her chair-bound husband would never do again.

The wife's positive input proved essential to the completion of the Brooklyn Bridge. Her father-in-law's original plans demanded technologies quite advanced for the time, and many an ordinary engineer, if called in, might have failed to finish as successfully the task she assumed when her husband lost the use of his body.

In the 1920s and long after, another Positive team of husband and wife had a powerful influence on the course of industrialization in America and around the world. Their contribution to scientific management of factories and offices is recognized and widely used to this day, but they are best known to the general public from the book written by two of their children, and the movie made from it. *Cheaper by the Dozen.*

Frank and Lillian Gilbreth indeed had twelve children, whom they raised with a lot of heart and rules concerning the "One Best Way" of doing things, which stemmed from their innovative time and motion studies of factory work. Their Positive Partnership worked in all areas of life. And when Frank died of a heart attack, Ullian continued their work for almost another fifty years, recognized as one of the world's leading industrial engineers long before her own death at ninety-four in 1972.

Her influence is still felt among us, far from factory and office, in our kitchens. For Lillian Moller Gilbreth, industrial engineer, also designed standards for efficient work-level countertops, kitchen cabinets that could be easily reached, and early food-processing appliances years in advance of their time.

The Boys from Grand Rapids

Not all Positive Partnerships are based on marriage or kinship. The most successful and long lasting business partnerships have a high quota of goal-sharing, Positive Thinking partners.

One well-known example is the lifelong friendship and partnership of two Michigan boys who decided in high school that they would like to go into business together.

They were not sure what business it should be, and they tried several before being almost forced, by a supplier company's failure to perform properly, to create the business known today as the Amway Corporation. It is perhaps the most dramatically successful—and enduring—multiple level marketing organization seen in the world since the birth of capitalism, though that may not have been what Rich DeVos and Jay Van Andel knew they were creating when they started in the DeVos basement.

Amway has a great many wife-and-husband teams in its distribution network. This I see as one hidden reason for its long success. The abundant energy from so much family enterprise, powered by the uncanny ability of Positive Partnerships to infuse ordinary people with extraordinary goals, drive, and persistence, explains a lot that appears on the plus side of the ledger without corresponding corporate cost on the other side.

I have met in my lifetime a handful of people who dislike—for whatever reason—all direct selling organizations, including Amway. But I confess to a fascination with a group that has figured a painless way to redirect money that's going to be spent anyway into the pockets of ordinary people willing to work hard and creatively for it, without diminishing the product or cheating the public.

The advertising, delivery, and other marketing costs for most goods we buy form a very large part of the final price we pay to the giant corporations that supply most of our needs. The genius of Amway, and its successful imitators, is the diversion of this expensive overhead, for certain products, out of high-cost conventional channels. Money that others must put into heavy advertising, multiple product sizes, regional warehousing, and full-shelf deliveries to every store in the country, Amway redirects into an independent 'networking' sales-and-delivery system... with ample rewards up and down the line for those who volunteer to make this novel, "only in America" kind of system work.

Positive Partnerships celebrated at the cultural level include collaborators of the musical stage, like Gilbert and Sullivan, Rodgers and Hart, and others. Popular literature captures the histories of other collaborators—scientific teams—that often are not recognized as the Positive Partnerships they are. For example, the work of Nobel winners James D. Watson, Francis Crick, and Maurice Wilkins as described in the bestseller, *The Double Helix,* recounting their detective story discovery of deoxyribonucleic acid (DNA) as the basic messenger of life, transmitter of all hereditary patterns.

At all levels, there are more Positive Partnerships out there than this world of ours has noticed. This might be because a lot of them are those devoted husband-wife teams whose partnership goals include the successful raising of a family, something done best in a quiet life. Two minds and one heart, sharing positive goals, do the quiet work that may make our future, though it never makes the news.

Positive Partners' Advantages

If there were only three ideas to be absorbed from Napoleon Hill's classic, *Think and Grow Rich,* the first would be: *Know what it is you want,* for all great achievements have their beginning in an idea.

No amount of Positive Thinking and no self-help book can help a person achieve something until that something is *clearly identified.*

The second idea would be: *Set a monetary measure to your goals,* for that is the only way to tell how close you are to them, as we have seen.

The third: *Form a Master Mind group* of persons who will offer their advice, counsel, and cooperation "in a spirit of perfect harmony." That is a tall order for most of us, getting a bunch of people to agree about anything. But Napoleon Hill did not say how big the group must be. For Hill's mentor, Andrew Carnegie, it was fifty well-paid men, whose wisdom was his whenever they convened. For my mentor. Art De-Moss, it was his wife Nancy, plus a bevy of advisors and consultants whom he paid a total of $250,000 a year... and wished he could find more to hire.

It need not be that complex. Most Positive Partners form their own Master Mind group, maybe bringing in one or two other closely involved people. The range of benefits are the same, and don't cost a fortune either.

What are these Positive Partner benefits, besides the extra mind that becomes available when you need a flow of good ideas or help in solving problems?

Prime would be the 360-degree vision field that is the benefit of any back-to-back partnership. You get more eyes looking out for impediments and opportunities. Things that might otherwise trip you up, or pass you by, have a better chance of being seen in time to act.

Second would be the division of responsibility that extra hands make possible. It's nice for the entrepreneur not to feel he must lash himself to the wheel so he doesn't part company with his ship while sleeping. Having a Positive Partner, when you can, makes work easier.

Third would be the mutual encouragement Positive Partners can give each other when adversity strikes, or moods are low or difficulties besetting.

Positive Thinkers are not immune to this life's problems. In fact, by creating new realities the way they do, they probably encounter a more than average number of work-related problems. But then they are given greater resources for resolving them.

The nice thing is, outside of work the "5 percent rule" does not apply. *Life's other problems are rather evenly distributed. If you're alive, you've got problems. Everybody gets their share. Yet the super-achieving 5 percent gets oily its fair share—not half— even while getting its normal half of life's extra rewards.* Which is something you might feel positive about.

Posi/Thoughts

The "extra mind" power generated by a Positive Partnership gives the team advantages over solitary workers. Positive Partnerships work best when they

1. know what they want
2. set monetary measures to their goals
3. form a working "master mind" group

The "5% Rule" applies only to what you do ... not to what gets done TO you. So Positive Thinkers may earn great riches but only get their normal share of problems outside the workplace.

*At the Risk
Of Hurting Yourself,
Never Believe in
Something More
Strongly
Than
The People
Who Are in
Charge of It.*

CHAPTER FOURTEEN

May The Positive Force Be With You!
Being a Plus in a Negative World

How does the Positive Thinker avoid being grounded out by negative attitudes and people sure to come his way?

It has never been easy. Positive Thinkers were always an endangered species, and little appreciated until this century. Even now they are not universally valued. If they were, you would not need this book. Every college would award degrees in the subject and every kindergarten would offer start-up classes. Instead of fond parents telling a child it could become president, they would seek first to make it a Positive Thinker. For its own benefit, and society's.

Each generation gets its share of Positive Thinkers, enough of them, if not suppressed, to lead that cohort to a better life. The record shows, however, that Positive Thinkers, despite their great value to society, have had—until very recent times—a discouraging way of being silenced, even killed off, by the groups among whom they lived. They were feared because they might foster change in cultures that stayed unchanged for uncounted generations.

In that long epoch when humans barely survived on this earth, whatever worked was valued. Fire worked. Stone tools worked. Familiar ways of trapping and killing animals for food and sinew and fur worked. Innovations might not work.

Or on the other hand, they might work so well as to entrap those who tried them. Suppose the new ways did work? Suppose everybody got dependent on them, food supplies increased, people started having more babies than before—and then something unknown went wrong? Everybody might die. Better not to take the risk. Better to kill the troublesome innovator. Or at least drive him out.

To be a Positive Thinker had life-shortening implications over most of our race's history.

Each generation gets its genetic quota of green-eyed beauties, freckled redheads, left handers, albinos, twins, born musicians, math geniuses... and its 5 percent of superachievers who are going to carry on half of that generation's creative work. We have been identifying in this group a high number of Positive Thinkers. And we act as if that were a good thing for all of us.

But it was not always so.

To be a conspicuous Positive Thinker in early times was about as safe as playing with saber-toothed tiger cubs outside the cave after dark with the fire out, the moon low, and mamma cat growling out by the clearing.

They're Not Playing Your Song

Only in fairly recent times, as industrialization and the mechanization of fanning gradually have made abundance possible for everybody, has Positive Thinking come into its own and out of social hiding.

We live in times of the most rapid change mankind has ever seen. And that suits Positive Thinkers just fine. Change is their native environment. They see it coming and help give it shape. They make it work for them.

But Positive Thinkers are not the majority. In the coffee of life, they are only the cream, enriching and lightening the rest of the cup. At least they don't get so many lumps these days.

As a minority, Positive Thinker/Achievers have to remember that *most of what they hear and read is NOT really directed at THEM!* It's aimed at the 95 percent majority whose ranks they have left. The majority is trying to keep its troops in line. That is what all the irrelevant palaver is about. Listen in if you must, but don't feel what you hear applies to you by name.

Most of what is said on television and radio, much of the guidance information in magazines, books, and papers, 99 percent of the experts telling people how to run their lives are simply not saying what Positive Thinkers need to hear! The stuff is worse than irrelevant. It distracts and misleads, blurring goals and making them harder to visualize and achieve in all the noise.

It's like visiting elementary school for the day as an adult. Bells ring, classes change, children chatter, teachers teach— but none of it really has anything to do with you. You are long past this stage in your life.

Those who adapt to the lifestyle of Positive Thinking need also adjust to the fact that they are strangers and pilgrims in their own land. The clamors of life, which so obsess the rest of the crowd, do not excite them. They heed other guides, beckoning up a path less traveled.

Once you internalize this truth, that no matter how average and unprepossessing they may appear, Positive Thinkers are a different breed, born to better choices, higher goals, and greater chances for success, then inner peace can take over. A shield of protective energy goes up around you, helping deflect the field of negativity that shorts out positive influences.

Giving Others Control over You

The first word most children learn to use is "NO!" There are good reasons for this. A child's speech capacity develops around the time it is discovering its own independence, its own existence as a separate person. A little negativity gives a little person a lot of control, as many a frazzled parent has found.

Yet behind it all, the child knows full well that if bad things start happening as a result of its forays into freedom, big people are still in control and will come to its rescue. It's part of a learning game, a stage we all go through.

Some never quite outgrow it. We see a lot of otherwise successful people tie velvet ropes around their own necks and hand the loose end to others. Down deep they seek to have someone else, some shadowy "big person" (who probably does not realize what role is so wistfully being attributed to him) take ultimate charge of their lives.

For a religiously committed person to do this, letting God hold the rope, is understandable. But letting a mere mortal like a board member, employer, client, creditor, colleague, or an in-law hold your rope is just to beg for them to give it a tug.

You put a rope around your *neck every time you ask other people to give unnecessary approval to what you do.*

In my professional work with nonprofit institutions I have seen self-lynchings frustrate wonderful plans that might have benefited thousands of needy people, had the plans been allowed to work. But the founder or chief executive had a weakness for approbation, a burning need for reiterated approval each step of the way. Instead of one nod from the board, dozens would be solicited, giving the project multiple opportunities to get canceled. Everything was done but to beg someone to choke the project. Naturally, somebody always took the hint.

An executive I know, an otherwise incisive leader of not-for-profit organizations, has a formidable record of establishing socially useful charities. Yet he finds himself continually foiled when he needs money. His fund-raising skills run to the low end of the scale, for he, like many, confuses publicity success with spendable income, which it is not. But he has an inborn talent to make money for himself in large chunks, a million at a time, by his own skills in selling.

So where is his money when he needs it, personally (since he is not too well paid by the charity), or when a new charity needs launching or a project needs help? Roped off, of course. He once assigned a near-million of his private earnings to the niggardly-hearted, negatively-bent board of a small religious denomination to whom he had also gratuitously granted title to a nonprofit group he created. He gave them a rope; why should they give him gratitude?

He wanted part of the money used to pay off the mortgage. The denominational board decided it might rather sell off the building (thus killing the charity because the location was essential to its mission) and pocket all the money, for the Lord's work of course. He has had to buy back the building several times now. His own money, brilliance, and energy have been used to fight him, wear him down, keep him from realizing the full effect of his considerable efforts.

And all he really wanted was for somebody to hold his velvet rope for him! He never expected them to tie it to a winch.

Jesus warned His followers about this when saying *"Cast not your pearls before swine."* Most people see the waste, but not the danger spoken of in the next verse: *"lest they turn and REND you."*

When Positive Thinker/Achievers *unnecessarily* let others control them or the fruit of their work, their gifts almost always will be perverted and used against them and the things they believe in.

This thought leads to another rule-of-thumb-in-the-eye: *Never believe in something more strongly than the people who are in charge.* This is not cynicism, just self-protection. The cynicism is usually on the part of the person in charge, in such cases, for not truly believing what the organization is all about. The overly-earnest junior employee (or outside consultant, as I often am) must not believe more intently in the group's mission than the person in charge. To persist where the leadership falters will cause them to hate you if you succeed. Most likely, they will use your sincere belief as a velvet rope to control and hurt you. They know where your interests lie and can try to frustrate them, negatizers that they are.

This brings up the "Use/Despise" Rule I apply to all my work, to keep from being shorted-out by negative people in organizations that express interest in my professional services. It goes like this: *"You may use me. Or you may despise me. But you cannot both use AND despise me."* If I find the leaders—or their circle of advisors—imbued with negative, pain-inflicting attitudes, I will not work with them. It would damage my other work.

Attracting Negative People

Then there are those negative people who will deliberately seek you out because they want to be positive like you. They form a hidden burden to Positive Achievers, for the attraction of your attitude and accomplishments agitate a longing in some would-be Positive Thinkers who have never quite made the grade.

They may slow you down. First with excessive admiration. Second with wanting you to take control of their lives.

It's a bit suffocating. Misleading as well. Without knowing better, you will want to help them, of course. And you probably should make the effort. Just be ready to cut yourself free if you see signs that they are practiced and perfected failures at everything you suggest they try.

Among the kind of client I turn down, when asked to help a charity overcome a bad deficit (the result of its previous mistakes), is the group that has had every known consultant through its place already. It is not really after advice or improvement. It merely likes to collect failure notices for its board of directors, the way a hypochondriac likes to baffle each new doctor who moves to town.

I can't let them waste my time. You can't spare the time either, if you have goals to achieve. None of us has any duty to live another person's life. Do your best, then walk away if you must. If someone draws true inspiration from your example, you will be happy to offer encouragement, naturally. Just beware the hang-on handful that hurts your time.

Changing certain friends and some activities may be the price you have to pay to preserve your Positive integrity in this overstimulating world where there is daily more of everything... except time in which to do it all.

When you are a true Positive Thinker/Achiever, the force Will, be with you. For you are that force.

Posi/Thoughts

Most of what goes on in the world is not meant for consumption by Positive Thinkers, who are only a minority of the population.

Positive people have no obligation to let others control them to their detriment.

Some negative people are attracted to Positive Achievers and will add to your burdens unless you avoid their influence.

Positive
Thinkers
Inherit
Tomorrow,
<u>Not</u>
Yesterday

CHAPTER FIFTEEN

The Payoffs of Positive Thinking:
Healthy, Wealthy... or Otherwise?

What, ultimately, are the benefits of Positive Thinking as a life philosophy? And are they worth the effort?

Let us address the ultimate payoff by asserting that the Positive Thinkers' goal-striving lifestyle may be the most *rational* way to live—and best way to thrive—in today's world.

In tomorrow's world, this will be even truer. The twenty-first century lies so close at hand, if it were a city, we would be driving through its suburbs right now. We approach this Third Millennium of Western Christian-rooted civilization laden with more population, hazards, and opportunities than we have ever seen. At a time like this, Positive Thinkers have a vital gift to share with their fellow passengers on this planet: themselves. They are valuable because *they bring purpose and rationality to our basically nonrational world.*

The calamities and disasters reported in the media each day do not give evidence of this being a logical, reasoning, rational world. If our behavior is media-driven (affected by the news) then what we do is based on irrational uncertainties, things beyond our understanding to control.

If this were a rational world, we could survive without newspapers, for there would be no such thing as news. Everything would be predictable. We might even get along without insurance companies, because they only help protect against uncertain outcomes, and there would be few of these.

If this were an orderly and predictable universe, earlier generations would not have taught children to say bedtime prayers with such shocking sentiments as "If I should DIE before I wake," because no midnight fire, sudden fever, falling tree, or madman would unexpectedly make off with a child's life.

IF ALL YOU DO IS REACT to what this unpredictable, irrational world throws at you. lacking positive plans and purposes of your *own to give direction to life, YOUR LIFE HAS NO RATIONAL PURPOSE beyond mere survival.* Animals and plants do as well, without the bother of dual brains, souls, and all that.

We must have purpose. Positive Thinkers get theirs from the goals they have chosen and strive toward daily. For as we saw in an earlier chapter, if we do not establish our own goals, someone else will set his up for us, and force us to bow down to them. At that point, we have already lost our freedom and a substantial part of our humanity.

Because Positive Thinking patterns foster our establishing worthwhile goals, they add meaning and purpose to life. That alone is a considerable benefit, easily worth the price.

Health vs. Wealth

Most of the time no one looks at life quite that deeply. People seem content to pursue Positive Thinking for two more immediate reasons—better health and greater wealth.

Health meaning well-being of body and mind. Wealth meaning an abundant accumulation of something or other. Not necessarily money. A person can be wealthy in friendships, rich with honors. Trace the word wealth back through our language and you find its meanings include happiness and its roots come from a word meaning to wish. All of which says—*wealth was originally perceived as a state of mind, not a condition of purse.*

From my privileged vantage point of almost twenty years, looking over Norman Vincent Peale's shoulder, so to speak, reading his mail and summaries of it at the Foundation for Christian living, I can say that of the millions who have written him for advice or prayer, most have been concerned with health.

Not merely obvious health concerns like cancer or recovery from heart disease, but alcohol and drug addiction as well, and healing of mental illness. Even letters from people seeking consolation over the loss of a loved one, or a person trying to overcome shyness or bad mental attitudes could be read as "health concern" mail, for they want that mental and physical well-being that we define as good health.

They also want their relationships healed. People write because they are lonely. Letters pour in concerning family. Damaged personal relationships are a continuing problem. Much of the damage, again, is health-related, some of it triggered by chemical abuse leading to child abuse and spouse abuse... and financial abuse.

Yet nobody sane and sober writes in saying, "Please tell me how to use Positive Thinking to get rich." They may ask prayer for their urgent financial problems, expressing confidence that they will be solved, as so often in their past. People will write about a family's need for a job or a raise.

No one writes in to say they want to be made rich, other than spiritually. Healthy, yes. Wealthy, no. Why is this?

In fact, if you analyzed Dr. Peale's prayer-request mail without knowing that it is virtually identical in content with that received by every visible religious institution from Billy Graham, on the Protestant side, to the National Shrine of Our Lady of the Snows, on the Catholic, you could be misled badly.

When I first started working with the Peaks, their staff believed the average person on their mailing list to be very old, very poor, of modest educational attainments, and sickly. This was far from true, and I knew it, from work with 200 other nonprofit organizations, and persuaded FCL to conduct a survey of donors and nondonors among the 600,000 families then requesting Dr. Peak's printed sermons.

What we found (and what I find true for all such groups) was this: *Those who are sick or in spiritual need write for prayer. Those who are well at the time do not ask for anything; they share. They send money.*

If you believed only the prayer mail, it would seem that Positive Thinking is for health, not wealth; a kind of spiritual Blue Cross, an aid in healing human hurts.

Only when you take in the larger picture, those significant voluntary gifts from large numbers of happy and healthy contributors, does it become clear these well people are saying Positive Thinking works for them. Feeling positive about their future, it is easy for them to be generous. They have or are on the way to having the wealth they want.

Positive Thinking as a Cure

Positive Thinking is no cure-all. The only thing it is guaranteed to cure is negative thinking. Even that is only by displacement, not direct assault, as we have seen.

Medically, its value is still being determined and the record is far from in. While science continues to explore mind-body links that may cause or cure disease, it is too soon to know what the link will prove to be. It may be weaker than we would like or stronger than we want to believe.

We have known since Bible days that "A merry heart doeth good like a medicine." But it cannot be said we have learned a lot more since then.

Though many find cause for encouragement in medicine's more open acceptance of the role of mind and attitude in keeping us well and restoring health, no one claims Positive Thinking is a guaranteed cure, though a well-known figure like writer Norman Cousins attests to the value of laughter and a positive mental attitude in allaying a serious disease that almost ended his life.

Until later years, even Dr. Peale had written surprisingly little about health after more than fifty years of nonstop publishing. People bring him their medical problems for prayer not simply because of his books on Positive Thinking, but because he is one of the preemiment clergymen of our century. His Foundation for Christian Living (Pawling, New York 12564) is a self-described Ministry by Mail to millions. Those who write there for prayer support might have written as readily to some other well-known pastor whose address was known to them. It is not the presumed healing power of Positive Thinking alone that draws them.

Positive Thinking's Most Common Use

By looking backstage at FCL I want to call attention to how sensibly the public deals with the utility of Positive Thinking. We also should note in passing that the mail generated by *Guideposts* magazine and other Peale media is not much different in content from that received at FCL, and reflects the same attitudes on the part of the public.

Advertising and book jacket blurbs aside, what do people actually use Positive Thinking for? In its fourth decade of public use it is fair to ask: What IS the *Power* of Positive Thinking?

It is a *Power* for health. For some it is a means they use, in addition to medicine, to enhance medical recovery or to forestall sickness. For a larger group, it is a way to brine injurious attitudes into line so as not to stress the body into illness. The true *Power* of Positive Thinking in medical practice may be negative... AVOIDING illness in the first place.

It is a *Power* for wealth. For some it opens insights into the reality of great abundance as an acceptable, attainable goal, if one is willing to pay its price and share its benefits. For many others, it opens the doors to realizing the basic wealth they dream of: A home, family, loved ones, useful work, and a happy place on the earth.

It is a *Power* to have power—the power to live life your own way, choosing the future that makes the most of your gifts, your goals, and your opportunities.

It is worth saying again. Positive Thinking may be the most rational way to live—and the best way to thrive—in today's world. And tomorrow's.

Posi/Thoughts

The lifestyle of the Positive Thinker tends toward a health of mind and spirit which is the wealth that most people seem to choose.

We Are
Born
<u>Optimists,</u>
Else Why
Do
Babies Smile?

CHAPTER SIXTEEN

Are You Positive?
Launching Your Positive Life-Plan

W*hen we are born, our parents give us our names, but THEY DO NOT TELL US WHO WE ARE.*

We spend our whole lives on a voyage of self-discovery: Who am I? What am I doing here? How am I supposed to do it? What if I don't want to?

Had we been born in another culture at another time, we might be expected to rename ourselves—several different times if need be—to reflect what it was we had become or wanted to be. To this day, nuns and monks, on taking their solemn vows, change personal names and drop family names to reflect and identify with ideals loftier than themselves.

The closest many Americans come to identification with the name of something greater than the self is when they don T-shirts or caps bearing the name or logo of some well-known corporation or its product. Brand loyalty as consumers— asserting what commercial products they identify with—is often their substitute for being whole people, describing themselves by what they buy, not what they do.

Whereas Indians of the Pacific Northwest identified themselves in tribal history with the legendary animals and birds shown carved on their totem poles, many of our contemporaries (if you believe what they wear) identify with beer or motor oil. Fashionable designer label clothes, boldly incorporating the designer's nametag or initials on the item worn, supply similar self-identification at other levels of society. We are all driven to identify ourselves with something greater than our selves.

Positive Thinker/Achievers identify strongly, not with things and social symbols, but with GOALS BEYOND THEMSELVES. In pursuit of those goals, they discover, on the way, their best and truest selves. They discover who they really are.

They also discover that the rules of Positive Thinking are few and simple, about like the fundamentals of driving an automobile: Drive in the right lane, use lights when you can't see, stay on the road, and don't hit anybody.

The unstated assumption is that you have somewhere in mind to go—a destination, a goal. And that is true for the Positive Thinker/Achiever as well, as we have seen. Your goals determine who and what you shall be, and where you are going with your life.

As we have also seen, the great thwarter of Positive Achievement is simply the failure to "turn on the key." Unless the engine is started, it does little good to fiddle with the gears or play with the wheel. No one is going anywhere until the "Positive Permission" key starts the motor.

It is my observation that fate favors those who are in motion. If moving in the wrong direction, they can readily be reaimed or redirected by a tilt of the cosmic table. Those not in motion are slow to overtake fast-moving opportunities.

Today Counts More Than Tomorrow

Life on our planet exists in a relatively thin film on the surface, confined roughly to a mile or so beneath the ocean and the same height above it. About the thickness of this book, compared to the Washington Monument.

Certain forms of animal and plant life themselves exist as thin boundary layers atop, or surrounding, earlier life, for example, coral and trees.

The coral animal lives a stationary existence fastened to the rocky remains of its predecessors. A coral reef may rise many feet from the ocean floor, but only the relatively thin top layer is inhabited with living coral. Likewise, only a small part of any tree is currently living.

The thin, wet layer between the bark and inner wood is, except for its energy-seizing leaves or needles, all that is truly alive on any tree, be it an apple seedling or a monumental redwood. Everything else beneath the bark is a relic of its past, a dead wooden column that supports new life.

Time, as we humans experience it, is like that thin film of life. Outside of it is the unexperienced future, inside is the assimilated past. Today only do we live and move and have our being.

We OWN the past, LEASE the present, and can only BORROW from the future. What we do each day, therefore, to reach our goals, is important to us. Time is not wasted, though we may waste time. We rebuild ourselves anew each day, by choice or by accident. Our lives are thin layers between past and future. Each day we make our history and our destiny. Positive Thinkers accept this and use it to their advantage.

Like personal computers, we reprogram ourselves each morning when we wake and start up for the day. We literally seem to reinstate our personalities, like so much computer software, each morning. If wise, we make improvements as we go along. Only by making gradual, daily shifts in our programming do we grow from wanting birthday toys at six to giving toys to our grandchildren at sixty. We make these subtle program shifts in response to our goals.

Life Is Mostly Small Decisions

Once you have your life-goals locked in place, you will find there are few big decisions that will ever confront you again. This is worth appreciating, for some people have demurred the Positive path, nagged by fear of constant pressure to make big decisions. But life is not so. Life is mostly small decisions, usually one stepping on the tail of another, each the natural consequence of earlier choices.

That is why each day is important to the Positive Thinker/ Achiever. Each small choice sets the way for further small choices, leading eventually to the goals that underlie the minor daily decisions.

Alcoholics Anonymous does not counsel troubled drinkers to make the big derision—never to touch another drop. Rather its success lies in teaching how to make a small choice—not to drink TODAY. Or if that's too hard, not to take a drink right this

Likewise, big goal decisions like succeeding in a business, or selling ten million dollars worth of insurance, once made, get replaced by much smaller decisions... like whether to get up that morning and go to work or sleep late. Repeated small decisions determine whether big goals get met. Today's small decisions are felt forever.

I once heard Rich DeVos, co-founder of Amway, assert that even during times of explosive growth he rarely felt compelled "to make major decisions; only a lot of little decisions." Big goals preset the small choices.

From rough marble, smooth statues emerge, the result of lots of little mallet taps on a chisel, reflecting lots of little decisions by the sculptor, who taps away everything that does not look like the model. The big decision—what to sculpt— was made before picking up the mallet.

Your One-Millisecond Manager

To the people who study such things, it now seems that our voluntary decisions are not made the way we thought. Much of our decision-making process is not under our conscious, knowing, control.

Our real inner decision is not "WHAT shall I do next?" but "Shall I do THIS specific thing or not?"

Our overt decisions are choices between accepting or rejecting specific, subconsciously prepared proposals for behavior. You may consciously want to reach for the stars, but your subconscious mind may ask if you first want to reach up and scratch your ear, because it itches.

Like a super-efficient secretary who anticipates most of the boss' needs and responses before he states them, our subconscious minds foresee expected needs and prepare menus of responses for us to choose from.

An easy example highlights what the researchers mean. You have just finished a leisurely Sunday afternoon nap and are lying on the couch waiting to get up. You are trying to decide when to swing your feet to the floor. One moment you are lying there, the next you are standing. Why?

If you think on it, you sense what these people are finding: You did not simply decide to get up and then just do it. Rather, *you said YES to some inner part of you* that had already proposed, several times, that you get up and get on with the day.

You did not rise sooner because earlier you said NO to the impulse. Now you said YES, and the action followed without conscious effort, already planned for you.

Most actions are taken after an inner vote on what the subconscious part of our mind proposes we do next. The nonverbal part of our brain suggests a course of action. A few milliseconds later the conscious, speaking part of our brain votes: yes or no?

If we say no, the unspoken thought remains but an impulse. If we say yes, it becomes action. But there is always this pause, this milliseconds-long break, during which we decide if the proposed action is right. In this interval our morals, conscience, and goals come into play. It is the hiatus that military training tries to close, demanding immediate, unthinking obedience.

We are human and not mere animals because we edit our impulses during these flickering fractions of a second. When temptation pops up, it is rarely delivered to us from the outside, hot off the prongs of a Satanic pitchfork. It's a familiar insider reintroduced by our uncritical super-secretary subconscious, which has a hunch we might like to give it a try. *(Now, Boss? Okay, Igor.)* To resist temptation is sometimes but to edit out bad ideas.

Like the talk show host on a radio phone-in program, we have our finger at all times on a cut-off button, to dump, in milliseconds, output that is not right for us.

This is the ultimate small decision for the Positive Thinker. There is none smaller or more important. Positive Thinking consists not in the banning of negative thoughts or bad suggestions from our subconscious—an impossible task—but in saying yes only to the right ones. The right ones are those that move us toward our consciously selected Positive goals.

Actions Precede and Cause Belief

The existence of the One-Millisecond Manager as an editor of our actions suggests where our conscience is located, and shows it to be more of a reactor than an actor.

It also says something about how we acquire and sustain our deepest beliefs, including our belief in the power of Positive Thinking to improve our lives and the world around us. It tells us *we act first,* then fully believe.

For if the impulse to action springs from subconscious, nonverbal parts of our being, so does the impulse to believe. Like the stage-mute comedian Harpo Marx, we act out our beliefs even if we can't say them.

Of course we saw all this some chapters back in discussing the AS-IF principle: *Act as if something is already true for you and you help it become so.* Positive belief in good health, love, and abundance helps make them realities even outsiders can recognize.

The physical act of affirmation confirms the choice the silent part of our mind makes. Once that choice is affirmed by action, it is now believed on both sides of the brain. Now we are free to work to actualize our belief.

Positive Is Not Perfect

It would be nice if Positive Thinking conferred perfection as well, but perfection is an unattainable goal on earth and is best left out of your Positive life plan, for its quest corrodes.

You have only to study the so-called perfect philosophical, political, and religious systems traced in history to see how they consume, if not the lives of their devotees, then their sanity. It is fine to idealize perfect political states, but foolish to insist we have the wisdom to bring one into existence. Humans are stuck dealing with the pretty good and not the perfect.

And so, apparently, is God, so long as He chooses to deal with us. By our human definitions, even the Deity is not perfect, because we have no adequate vocabulary to describe Him. For instance, we say of someone who lacks artistic ability, "He can't even draw a straight line," as though that were the mark of a competent artist.

Consider then, the Creator has never been known to draw a straight line anywhere, in the entire history of our universe, no matter how many light-years we look into space or how deep we look into the ground.

God chooses not to deal in straight lines. We do. Is He any less perfect for that? Everything in nature curves, including light rays, waterfalls, shorelines, tree trunks, fox trails, and beelines. The shortest distance between two distant points on our globe is not a straight line but the curve of a great circle route. When you look down from a plane you can always tell man's handiwork from God's. If it is full of straight lines you know it is something man-made, a railroad, canal, power line, city, or farm.

Everything God touches curves. In sending to earth His Son Jesus, as Christians believe, God "threw a curve" at us. for it was an unexpected maneuver to say the least. The Devil would have been more linear, like us, saying "Here I am. Worship me." Jesus spoke mostly in parables, stories which, like parabolas (same root word) touch us at one place and curve off quickly in another direction, usually God's.

If we can't make God fit our standards of perfection enough to make straight lines, I say we have no business imposing perfectionist systems on anyone—including ourselves.

And that brings us, by a curved route, back to Positive Thinking.

Don't be disappointed if it only makes life great or pretty good and not perfect. Save something for Heaven.

Above all, don't think you have failed because negative possibilities cross your mind, or an occasional fear takes on worry status.

Positive Thinking aids life, is life at its best, though life is not perfect. But if not perfect, life is indomitable, despite every change.

You Have What It Takes

Change is something Positive Thinkers cope with, better than the 95 percenters do. They sense it coming. They may not like what change brings, but they accept it the way birds accept wind, fish accept waves. They move with it. If they go under, they are likely to come out on top.

They find ways to change change itself to their benefit and liking. They form the cutting edge of creativity, the growing edge of faith. They have what it takes. And so do you.

All along I have been saying that "5 percent of the people make 50 percent of our gains," and demonstrating that rarely considered truth in different ways. But that 5 percent is not an aristocracy of birth, whose privileges are denied to the less favored. *Positive Thinkers are an aristocracy of CHOICE.* They chose to become what they are... and will be.

So can you. You already are what you have chosen to be, so far. You have the Positive power to choose to go higher if you but give yourself permission to climb.

If you never had permission before, you have it now.

Posi/Thoughts

Today is the most important day the Positive Thinker will ever live.

The great things in life are reached mostly through many small decisions. Our Positive goals help us make those decisions.

We "reprogram" our personalities every morning, and this lets us make daily small choices in the direction of our ultimate goals.

Perfectionism is not the purpose of Positive Thinking; constructive goal-reaching is.

You have what it takes to succeed.

Why not get started right now?

POSITIVE
SCRIPTS

My Positive Permission

As a valid human being made in the image of God, you come with built-in authority to reach every goal you can.

If your inner authority—permission—has not been fed by example, credential, education or outside authority, find it for yourself by writing out the following affirmation and making it your own (see page 55).

Carry it with you and affirm it into your deepest subconscious mind.

My Goal-Imaging Script

Outline, on as much paper as you need, the self-written "inner TV Script" of your goals, to play back in your imagination again and again until your subconscious mind accepts them as real goals it is to achieve in the real world.

Your goal script features you as the hero, shows your goals as achieved or in the process, and is vivid with detail. It is a film-clip of your coming success, a scrapbook page snatched from history before it happens.

See it. Taste it. Smell it. Hear it. Feel it. By replaying your soon-to-be-true story against the back of your eyeballs many times a day, your whole being will soon joyfully focus on achieving your specific, life-enhancing, measurable goals.

MY POSITIVE LIFE PLAN

1 My Positive Life Purpose. (What I wilt do with the n of my life.)

☐Simple ☐Clear ☐All-encompassing

MY POSITIVE LIFE PLAN

2 My Positive Life-Coals. (What I will give in exchange for what I get.)

☐Specific ☐Life-enhancing ☐Measurable

My Positive Life Plan

3 My Positive Time-Frame. *(How soon can I expect to set results; how long will they continue.)*

☐Months ☐Years ☐Lifetime ☐Beyond

My Positive Life Plan

4 My Positive Measure of Success. *(How I will know when my goals are reached.)*

☐Money ☐Measurable Attainment